All These Days

January Kelly

Edited by: Kymmee E'light Beiger

Cover design: Black Widow Designs

DEDICATION

For Gail, Bobbye, and Pam
Three uniquely amazing women that I had the deep
pleasure of knowing, loving, and calling Mom.

Here I sit all alone like an airplane
On the edge of a sky full of solid gray
Staring at the ceiling, tell me that I'm dreaming
Oh, I wish you were here today
All these days I know I'll never get back
All these words I know I wish I should've said
All these dreams that we had now fade to black…

--Leigh Kakaty

1

February 12

Cancer.

He just said the word. This most beautiful, broad man with dark chocolate skin and a smooth Senegalese accent just said the most hateful word in the English language: cancer. I stared blankly at the painted cinder block wall in front of me. I could hardly breathe; but if I were being honest, I really shouldn't have been shocked. She had been a smoker since she was a teenager and even on oxygen now, she still found herself craving one.

"Are you okay, ma'am?" Dr. Mbaye said politely.

I shook the cobwebs out of my head, "Oh, yeah…I'm fine."

I looked over at my mother. I figured she probably didn't hear a word he had said. A severe ear infection as a child had taken most of the hearing from her right ear and age had taken most of it from the left. Also, she refused to wear the hearing aids she had purchased the year prior. She was a bit stubborn.

"So," I continued, "You called it…what kind of cancer, again?"

"Small cell carcinoma in the upper quadrant of the right lung," he replied.

"And what are our treatment options?" I asked and glanced back at mom who was sitting very still with her eyes closed.

Dr. Mbaye touched my mother's knee and spoke a little louder, "Miss Evelyn?"

My mother's piercing blue eyes opened, and she smiled sweetly at him.

"Miss Evelyn, we have a few things we can do to treat this. There is chemotherapy and radiation. Are you interested in any of those?"

My mother stared at him for a moment, which apparently made him think for a split second that she didn't understand what he said. He looked for me to assist, but I waited; I knew she was processing.

"Well," her voice was clear as she spoke, "I don't want any of that chemotherapy. I'm almost eighty-three years old and I'm not spending what time I have left with my head in a damn puke bucket."

Dr. Mbaye smiled at her, "I understand and that is one hundred percent your decision."

"So," she continued as she cut him short, "What else you got, handsome?"

The tall, beautiful man's laughter filled the room, "Yes, ma'am. Well, we can do specialized radiation that targets the exact spot of the tumor. You would come here, to the hospital every other day, for two weeks and get five treatments total."

My mother looked at me and shrugged. What she was saying was *"What do you think, kid?"*

I had been my mother's sole caretaker for the past seven months as multiple sclerosis and emphysema had begun to steal away her strength and the ability to take care of herself. We had developed our own sort of shorthand when it came to communication, and it was one she preferred when in the presence of medical personnel.

I nodded to her, "I think that sounds reasonable." I turned back to the doctor, "As long as it won't make her sick?"

"No," he shook his head and touched her knee again, "I promise, you won't be sick. If you are, I'll let you punch me."

The comment elicited an enormous grin from my mother, "Oh, I would never…"

Her sapphire eyes batted at him as she patted his hand.

She is such a flirt.

Dr. Mbaye turned back to me, "I'll put in the request and scheduling will call you by Friday. She'll need to come back next week to be fitted for the vest she'll wear…it's made just for her and helps the machine locate the exact spot to treat. After that, we should be good to go."

"Thank you so much, doctor," I sighed. I was actually relieved a little knowing that she would agree to some sort of treatment. I already knew her aversion to any type of chemotherapy as she had already voiced her opinion on the matter. Giving her opinion was also something she was very good at doing.

He turned back to my mother as he rose from the short, round rolling stool where he sat, "Miss Evelyn, we caught this early. Earlier than we usually do, I think this treatment will do pretty well for you. You are a rare bird, indeed."

He shook her hand then opened the door and stood back for me to wheel her out of the room. She was quiet as I rolled her down the lengthy, stark white hall of the oncology center. I stopped at the front desk and scheduled her follow-up. I then rolled her to the parking lot and to the edge of my six-year-old silver Tahoe.

Using the inside handle of the door, Mom pulled herself to her full five feet to allow me to load her wheelchair in the back. When I returned to the door, I pulled out the small wooden step stool and placed it on the ground in front of her. She stepped onto the stool then raised her left leg and placed it inside the vehicle. With my left arm and shoulder, I got close to her and gently lifted and pushed her rear end into the seat. I snapped her seat belt, shut the door, and returned the stool to the floorboard behind her.

It's a unique workout.

"Is it lunchtime?" She asked as her familiar ornery grin spread across her face.

She loves to go out to lunch on appointment days.

I clicked my seat belt across my chest, "Of course! What are we having today? Mexican? Hamburgers?"

"Breakfast," she stated emphatically.

I grinned to myself as I knew that would be her answer.

My mother lived with me, my husband, and our two high school-aged children in a large two-story, four-bedroom home that my husband and I had built on a couple of acres of land we purchased right after we were married. We had always imagined that one of our parents would be living with us in the future so as it were, we built our guest room on the bottom floor with its own en suite bathroom and outdoor access. This decision worked out quite well, as my mother was still able to maintain a little independence because of it. After getting Mom to her bedroom for a nap, I decided it was probably a good time, while I had the chance, to call my brother, Remy.

I actually have two brothers, one older named Jack, and my twin brother, Jeremy. For obvious reasons, I've always been closer to Remy. That's not to say that I didn't have a relationship with my older brother, but I've always found him to be a pushy, know-it-all, so our togetherness has always been strained. Our mother always wanted the three of us to "get along", using her words, so we do our best to remain cordial in her presence which usually means Jack has to bite his lip and keep his unwanted comments to himself. I find immense pleasure in that, but my humor has always been a little dark.

I let the phone ring once. Twice. Three times. I am about to hang up when I hear my brother's quick greeting.

"Hey! What's up?" he asked cheerfully.

"Hey Remy…you busy?" I ask.

Remy is a traveling welder for a third party that holds contracts for upkeep on oil lines. He makes great money and is able to fill his deep-seeded need for adventure and travel. He's always had a bad case of wanderlust.

"No, I just put up early for the night. You?" his voice was still cheerful.

I sigh, "Mmm, we probably should talk."

I heard him crack a beer and take a pull.

"That doesn't sound good… Hit me with it," his voice became heavy.

"She's got cancer, Rem," I tried to repeat exactly what the doctor had told me earlier that day. "Small cell carcinoma in the upper quadrant of the right lung."

"Damn," Remy paused, "Treatment?"

I shook my head as if he could see me, "No chemo… Mom refuses. But she agreed to targeted radiation…I'll take her in for five days over two weeks, then we'll see."

"Fuckin' cigarettes man," he said.

"Yeah, well, we'd be having a different conversation right now if you hadn't quit," I chided him.

He took another pull of beer, "Well, I did… All your nagging worked."

I had to laugh to myself. I've always thought smoking was a nasty habit and I had bothered him for years to quit. That was my birthday present four years ago from Remy.

Best gift ever.

"Jer, do you need anything?" he asked.

I laughed wildly, "A half dozen whiskey sours and a week in Barbados should do the trick."

"Well, I've got two ultra-light beers and a view of some very pretty rocks," he offered tongue-in-cheek.

"Pass," I replied.

"Can't say I didn't offer."

I could almost hear his shoulders shrug; I knew my brother.

"How long until you're home?" I asked. I needed help and my twin was the only person besides my husband I could count on for support. Remy didn't like being tied down for long, two divorces proved that, but I knew he would drop everything and forgo his nomadic life if I asked.

"I'll be back in a couple weeks, I can stay a week or

so, then back on the road," he replied.

"Okay, that will work," I said as strongly as I could. I would have preferred it if he could have been home sooner, but I would take what I could get.

"You tell Jack-ass yet?" Remy asked referring to our older brother.

I had to giggle at his choice of nickname tonight, "Fuck. No…I've been putting it off. I called you first…I'm not sure I'm in the right mental head space to deal with him right now."

"Rip off that band-aid. And whatever you do, make sure he knows you called me first," he laughed.

"You're a troublemaker, Rem," I chuckled at my brother.

"Look, you and I both know that he's not going to do or say anything to be helpful. I say fuck him," he commented.

"I can't do that Rem…you know mom, she just wants us to get along," I replied.

Remy snapped back, "Yeah, well, mom needs to live in reality."

"I know," I sighed.

I really didn't want to have this haggard argument again with him. If Remy had his way, neither of us would speak to Jack ever again. I understood his position; Jack was nothing short of a nightmare most of the time. He was a blowhard. An arrogant, pompous, eternally perfect, self-righteous, piece of work. He had made some money in his life and married into it, twice. The third marriage was apparently for love as they had been together longer than either of the first two combined. She was a sweet woman that worked for the highway department as a project director. She was smart, kind, and funny; and for the life of my twin and I, we couldn't begin to understand why she was with Jack.

Jack was also very lucky in the financial department. He made some good investment decisions early in his career and was able to sell his lucrative accounting business and retire early. Something he liked to rub in Remy's face from time to time. Remy went to a technical school and learned to be a welder; Jack went to college and got a degree. Remy was married twice but neither marriage produced any children; Jack had married three times and had three kids. Remy enjoyed the occasional beer or even a toke or two of sacred herb; Jack didn't smoke, drink, chew, or associate with those who do. I remember the day Remy came home and told the family what he wanted to do with his life.

***

Mom and Dad were sitting in their matching recliners watching television; most likely some sort of police drama because it was Mom's favorite. I, still elated from finding out that Rhett would be home for two weeks right after the new year, was busy talking on the phone to Holly. I heard my twin brother's old, beat-up truck from the next block as he made his way home from work. I ended my call with Holly just as Remy and Jack walked through the front door.

"Boys!" Mom called out.

"Hey Mom," Jack remarked, "Kathleen needs to borrow your sewing machine…that's okay, right?"

Mom jumped up, crushing out her cigarette, "Sure! Let me get it in the carry case…" And she left the room.

"Hey Pops," Jack patted Dad's shoulder as he walked by, following our Mother to the family room.

"You tell them yet?" I whispered to Remy. He gave me a small twitch of his head toward the left. We had almost a secret code of sorts, Remy and me. We used a lot of non-verbal communication, sort of our own personal twin sign language. That small movement meant, "*No, not yet.*"

Jack and Mom reentered the living room and Jack asked, "Tell them what?"

Remy's eyes rolled and Mom's brow furrowed in his direction.

"Oh, Jeremy…stop with the ugly face. Tell us what?" she ordered in her sweet but commanding way.

"It's nothin' Mom…it can wait," he did his best to deflect. Remy knew that the minute he said anything, Jack would have an unsolicited opinion because he couldn't help himself.

Jack shoved Remy's shoulder as he walked by, "Mom asked you a question, *Jeremy.*"

The words were condescending and more of an order than a statement.

"It's nothing…I just…I've decided that I'm going to welding school in Warrensburg…I've already applied and even got a scholarship," my brother shrugged modestly.

Mom and Dad simultaneously cheered.

"That's fantastic!"

"Way to go, son…"

"So proud of you!"

Jack began to laugh hysterically.

"What's so funny?" I demanded.

He took a gasping breath, "A *welder?* God, you really are a loser…"

Jack continued to laugh.

"You're a jerk, Jack," I remarked. I would have said

something a lot more colorful, but I was afraid to in front of our parents.

Remy glared, "Whatever, asshole."

Clearly, Remy didn't care that our parents were in the room.

"Ah! Jeremy Andrew…none of that out of you," Mom warned then turned to Jack, "And you stop giving him a hard time…there is nothing wrong with doing manual labor. I think it's wonderful."

She turned her back on my eldest brother, so she didn't see his face when he mouthed under his breath, "Oh, okay Mom…sure."

***

When Jack wasn't making snarky remarks about Remy's lifestyle, he turned his unwarranted comments to me. My natural response to Jack had always been to tell him to fuck off, if Mom and Dad weren't around, of course. I honestly couldn't give a shit what he thought of me. It was something I had to learn though. Jack looked at me like the baby sister he needed to protect; I looked at Jack like the pain in the ass he was. He hated that I defended Remy in everything.

"You're too smart for that…"
"You're educated like me…"
"That kid is a loser…"

Yep, fuck off Jack.

He was right, I am one of the thirty-eight percent of Americans that have a bachelor's degree. I always wanted to be a teacher, but not just any kind of teacher. No. I wanted to be the teacher that all the kids talked about years after graduation when they reminisced about their good old days with their children, much like our Dad. I wanted to inspire kids to become whatever the hell they wanted to be; I wanted to make a difference in someone's life.

So, I became an English teacher.

Yeah, I know. No kid ever looks back fondly on the one educator that pushed them to use proper punctuation or read a classic but, I love teaching…or I should say *loved* teaching. After my dad died, of cancer, the colon kind, my mom was left to pick up the pieces of her life without him. For a while, she had no idea how to function; he was her best friend. Even the simple act of going to the grocery store brought with it fountains of tears when she realized she didn't need to buy two gallons of milk when a half gallon would suffice. Then her own health began to deteriorate dramatically. Her walking became unsteady, and she would complain that her left leg and side would go numb. After two months of testing and six months after the death of my father, we learned she had late onset Multiple Sclerosis. I remember the day that diagnosis came and much like this cancer, it's not something I'll likely forget.

***

Mom called us to her house one Sunday afternoon for lunch. The three of us knew immediately that something was different with this day because she asked that only we show up and not our extended families. I was the first to arrive and begged her to tell me what was wrong. She only smiled at me saying, "We'll wait for your brothers."

Remy was the next to arrive, followed by Jack, who,

per his usual standard, was thirty minutes late. He calls it *casual etiquette*; I call it rude. Once we all gathered around the dining room table with plates full of smoked ham and twice-baked potatoes, Mom cleared her throat to get our attention.

"Well, I'm sure you're wondering why I asked you all to lunch today," she nodded in my direction.

The anticipation felt like a vice on my entire body, and I certainly wasn't hungry.

"I had an appointment with Dr. Martinez on Friday, and he confirmed I have late-onset MS," she explained plainly.

My heart sank. She had been having issues for several months with numbness in her limbs and pain. This wasn't good news. I looked over to Remy and watched his brow furrow as he tried to assimilate the new information. I glanced in Jack's direction and saw the wheels in his head begin to turn. I had seen this countless times before; my brother's analytical mind was engaging. Ever since we were children, Jack always had an uncanny ability to make every situation a way of asserting his dominance in the most calculated way possible. It came as easy and as naturally to him as breathing. If there was something in this for him, he'd find a way to exploit it.

"What does that mean, exactly?" he asked pointedly.

Our mother chewed her food thoughtfully for a moment. "Well son, it means that my body is attacking itself…it's the cause of the muscle pain and numbness in my arms and legs…also why I am so exhausted sometimes." She shrugged, "But, now I know it's not all in my head…and of course, there's treatment for it."

"Treatment? Like what?" he continued.

Mom waved her hand dismissively, "Oh…all kinds. Joel is going to start me on an immunosuppressive and I'll start physical therapy…we'll see how that goes.

She took another bite of food.

I watched Jack's face and knew what his next question would be before he even asked.

"How much is that going to cost, Mom?"

Money. Everything came down to two things for Jack: Money and his perceived power.

"I have insurance, Jackson," was her reply.

The tears had already welled in my eyes before I could stop them, and Jack pounced on me like a jungle cat.

"Oh Jesus…waterworks already, Jer?" he laughed at me.

I wiped my tears quickly and coughed. I wasn't usually like this, but I was only two weeks postpartum with Harrison and our mother just told us she had an incurable, debilitating disease. I felt I had a right to those tears.

"Eat shit, Jack," I growled.

He laughed again, "That's clever…good comeback."

"Just knock it off, Jack," Remy warned.

"Who the hell is talking to you, loser? The adults are speaking," Jack snapped.

Remy rolled his eyes but remained quiet for the moment. I narrowed my gaze on my oldest brother.

"Why are you so concerned about how much the treatments will cost?" I asked.

"What are you talking about?" Jack replied.

"You seem real worried about how much this will cost…a normal person would ask about how she's feeling… not about money. You worried about an inheritance?" I was long over my brother's bullshit and felt no shame when calling him to the mat.

"No, Jera," his tone now condescending, "I just want to make sure there's enough for her living arrangements."

"Living arrangements!? What the hell are you talking about?" Remy barked.

"She's disabled, dumbass…she'll be moving somewhere that can take care of her…"

"Disabled?!" I cut him off, "She looks pretty capable to me…"

Jack's voice rose, "…she needs somewhere she can be looked after…"

"Oh, get bent, Jack," Remy yelled.

"Jack! Jesus Christ..I think she can make her own…."

"You two need to stay out of this! I'll be deciding what happens and I'll find her a place…cared for…"

The room devolved into a cacophony of interruptions and raised emotions.

"Enough! From all of you!" Mom's voice carried over the room and hung in the air. "I just don't understand why we can't sit down at this table and have one goddamn meal!" Her fists hit the table.

I hung my head, nodding gently because I knew she was right. At the best of times, it took all of our own extended families to be in attendance for us to act civil toward each other. It had been that way since we were adolescents. I can't even pinpoint the exact moment when we stopped getting along or if we ever did. Most of my memories were of Jack locking Remy and me out of the house for hours on end while we baked in the sweltering Missouri summer heat. Which, if I'm being honest, Rem and I preferred anyway. We would ride our bikes all over the neighborhood and then stop at a little convenience store for cheap candy and soda. Eighties kids: we lived a life of unsupervised freedom.

I remember Jack always being a bully of sorts. One distinct memory is him punching Remy so hard in the chest that he lost his air for what felt like forever; I thought he was dying. Rem always took most of the abuse from Jack. That wasn't to say that I didn't get my fair share, he did put my head through a glass window one time, I *think* by accident. He was smart enough not to get caught most of the time, but he also knew if our Dad caught him picking on me, the lone daughter, the punishment would be unimaginable.

So, in his infinite wisdom, my older brother suggested that Mom might consider going into a home where she could be cared for and watched over.

She was sixty-five years old.

Fuck off, Jack.

Luckily, she continued to care for herself at home for several more years. She took her medicine, went to therapy, and generally followed all the rules…except, of course, for the smoking. No way in hell she was giving that up. When she was seventy-two, she came down with pneumonia that put her in the hospital for two solid weeks. She went in deathly ill…she came out with an emphysema diagnosis and oxygen. Jack raised concerns again that she was too frail to be left alone and that she should pay for a nurse to come in and stay with her or maybe a home where she could be cared for and watched over. It was the same tired argument from years earlier. But instead of allowing the conversation to become a screaming match again, I made the choice to become her caretaker. She didn't need full-time care, but some help around the house wouldn't hurt. I would somehow make it work with my schedule so she could stay in her home.

Fuck off, Jack.

The day that I called the ambulance to come to pick our mother up from her home because her lips were blue was the same day that my husband, Rhett, and I broke ground on the original plan for our new home. We had lived a fairly modest life for most of our marriage and had purchased a three-acre piece of property two miles outside of the city. We spent a couple of years clearing a nice spot in the middle of the wooded area we now owned to make room for our forever home. The well had been drilled and the backhoe was on site when I called Rhett to tell them they were admitting mom.

"I think it's time for Plan B," he said.

"Are you serious? I mean…I know it's something we talked about but, are you sure we can swing that? Aren't the plans all ready to go?" I replied.

"Babe, it's your Mom. We knew this was probably in our future…it will be fine. Besides, you know what Jack is going to suggest."

Oh, I knew: A home where she could be cared for and watched over.

Fuck off, Jack.

We broke ground and my wonderful husband submitted a new plan set to our contractor. We would have room for us, our two teenage children, and a large bottom-floor guest suite that would soon house a very special guest. At the end of the summer, when the house was ready, we brought my mom over for a tour. She ooo'd and ahhh'd at how spacious the kitchen was. She commented on the large family room and even made a great suggestion on where we should put the Christmas tree that year. But when we made our way into the larger of the two bedrooms on the first floor, she was confused.

"Why would you put your master bedroom down here? Are you giving the kids the whole second story?" she asked.

I giggled as Rhett winked at me.

"No, mom," I replied, "This is a guest room. See? And it has its own bathroom with a walk-in shower."

She looked around the bathroom, "Well, I do like your taste in color…those pink curtains are beautiful. But… you could almost live in this bedroom. Jera, this is huge…honey, it's almost a waste of space," she frowned.

"Well, we were thinking, when you're ready that maybe *you* could live in this room," I offered.

My mom looked from my husband back to me.

"What?" she asked.

"Mama E," my husband said as he squatted to look her in the eye, "When you get tired of talking to yourself in that big house of yours, you've got this room and this bathroom with the pink curtains waiting for you."

Her mouth fell open, "Are you serious? You didn't do this for me! And I don't talk to myself all of the time…I talk to Beegee too."

Baby Girl or 'Beegee' was my mom's Sheltie. My dad had given her as a gift to my mother a few months before he died, and Mom felt like she had a direct line to my dad as long as Beegee was around.

Rhett laughed and we both smiled at her, nodding. My mom began to cry.

They weren't tears of sadness but of joy. She had been so lonely after my dad had passed that she barely left her house at all anymore. Rhett and I tried to visit as often as we could on top of the evenings that I spent taking her shopping or cleaning her house, but with our schedules and the kid's schedules, sometimes, and I'm not ashamed to admit this, it was a real chore. Rhett had suggested at one point that I ask Jack to help out so I could have a break once in a while, even though he knew my brother's help would never happen. Jack might call Mom every couple of weeks, but to come by and spend a few hours vacuuming a floor or making a meal? Laughable. Even Remy, who worked over the road, saw Mom more than Jack did. There were times I didn't even know my twin was in town until I pulled into her driveway and saw his truck there. I knew she needed more attention but there just weren't enough hours in the day and I couldn't change that. But that didn't mean I didn't feel guilty. It also didn't mean I didn't try.

Which is more than I can say for Jack.

***

"No, Jack…the doctor thinks that this radiation treatment will be fine," I said exasperated, pacing the room.

Rhett looked at me from across the dining room table where he sat grading papers.

"Well, she needs to do the chemotherapy… You need to *make* her do it," he countered.

"*Make* her do it? For fucks sake … how am I supposed to do that, Jack? You *have* met our mother, right?" I asked angrily and threw my hands up in the air at my husband. He rolled his eyes and made a slash with his hand across his throat; his sign to me to cut the conversation off.

"All I'm saying *Jera* is that she isn't thinking straight, you don't know what that MS has done to her mind," he replied.

I rolled my eyes again, "Jack, I'm very clear on what MS has done to her brain… Nothing. She is as sharp as she's always been…her body is broken Jack, not her mind."

"Well, you're just giving up," his voice was becoming testy.

"Oh, screw you, Jack…I'm not having this conversation with you. I told Rem I shouldn't call you tonight," I bit back.

I knew how to hit below the belt.

Jack was quiet for a moment, "I see. So, the loser brother gets to know everything first…that's nice Jer."

"Whatever. I gotta go…our mother, you know, the one that I gave up my career to take care of full time, needs me. Later Jack."

I hung up the phone.

"I'm not sure why you let him get to you like that," Rhett commented over the piles of ungraded assignments, his steel blue eyes looking into my soul.

I glared at my husband, but he was right. I had allowed Jack to get under my skin. He had a particular way of placing himself above other people and making you feel like a complete moron. I loathed how smug he was all the time. But I learned to tolerate him because I loved our mother. Sometimes I wondered if he did. I had to practically beg him to come to see her most of the time and when he did, he might stay thirty minutes. I didn't mind his short visits, but I could tell it hurt mom's feelings; all she wanted was to spend as much time as she could with her children and grandchildren.

I finished prepping Mom's dinner, placed it on the old metal tray she liked, and delivered it to her in the living room as Beegee waited for scraps at her feet. This is how we ate a lot of meals. Rhett, surrounded by assignments he's grading, while picking at a plate of food in the dining room. Mom, seated comfortably in her pale blue, electric recliner in front of the television, and me helping myself to a spoonful or two as I made sure everyone's plates were full. Tonight, like most nights, neither of our children was home for the evening meal. Harrison, our eldest had basketball practice until four-thirty, then off to work at a chain burger restaurant by five. For Stacia, it was basketball then working at a different fast-food joint. Rhett and I were so lucky to have the children we had; smart, responsible, and for the most part, they stayed out of trouble.

As soon as I knew Mom was comfortably enjoying her dinner, I returned to the office upstairs and continued with my call list. There were several family members, other than my brothers I would need to call and let them know about Mom's new diagnosis. On my Dad's side, I had my Aunt Leann, his brother's wife, then his sisters, Aunt Jean, and Aunt Patty. Mom's side was a much shorter list, just one sister, my Aunt Yvonne. Once I checked all of them off, I made one final phone call to my best girlfriend, Holly.

"Did you call Jack?" she asked.

I groaned, "Yes, of course."

"Before or after Rem?" she snickered.

"After. And once his asshole started to show, I let him know it too," I replied, reaching over for a can of Diet Coke. I wasn't sure how long it had been there today, but right now, I didn't care.

Holly laughed heartily in my ear, "Good job!"

"Yeah, well…Goddamn it Holl…why does he have to be like that?" I charged.

"Jack's always been a dick. So what? Fuck him," Holly replied.

"But I just don't understand *why* he's like this…we were raised by the same parents in the same household. How did he turn out like that…all goddamn self-important," I said.

"Who knows? But don't let him stress you out…you've got enough to handle. Speaking of, how did Mom take the news?" she asked.

I sighed, "Pretty well, I guess. You know her, she didn't say a lot," I replied.

Holly laughed, "Did she *hear* the diagnosis?"

That was the point I broke into an uncontrollable fit of giggles. It felt so good to laugh like that.

When I was able to catch my breath, I said, "Yeah…but again, you know her…the doctor was cute, so she flirted a little."

"Of course, she did…so, what happens now?" she asked.

"Five days of radiation…then, we'll see, I guess. She's refusing chemo," I answered.

"You knew she would…your dad was so sick from it…she's not gonna put herself through that. And Jer, who could blame her? She's eighty-two! Goddamn…if I make it that long, and they want to give me that crap, I'd say fuck all too," Holly replied.

She was right and I had to agree with her. I can only hope that I make it to live to be in my eighties, I'd be damn lucky if I did. Hell, maybe I'd like to see ninety. Holly and I could share a room in a nursing home, watch talk shows, and fight over pudding. And when the doctors came to tell me I had some horrible disease, I'd say, "Fuck all!" and dive from my wheelchair naked into the fountain out front.

A girl needs a dream.

2

February 19

A week later, I unloaded Mom from the Tahoe and back into her wheelchair, to make our way down the long, white-washed hallways of the Johnson Regional Hospital Oncology Center. After calling her name, a very young nurse came out and took her back to the radiology room and prepped her for her vest fitting. They were gone about an hour as I waited in the small, windowless room with the bland waiting room seating and stale decor when the same nurse rolled her back out.

"Thank you, Sarah,…see you next week!" my mother smiled wide then looked up at me as I took over the wheeling duties. "That's a sweet girl right there…Sarah. She might look little, but she's a tough one…I sat on that table and she just…"

Mom made a sweeping motion with her hands.

"Tossed my legs up on that table like it was nothing. And! It's a robot, Jera! They've got a robot doing all the work on my old lung…they didn't have anything that advanced when I worked. I don't like being strapped to that table though…" she continued.

"Wow! That's great Mom…don't worry about being strapped down…it's only for like five minutes…they need you to be really still," I assured her.

"Oh, I know…but...ach..." she shivered. "It's horrible."

I wheeled her out and put her back into the truck. It was close enough to lunch that we stopped at Mom's favorite diner to eat. She ordered her usual of two over-medium eggs, two slices of crisp bacon, hash browns, and toast. I drank coffee and had an English muffin.

"You need to have more than that," she frowned at my small plate.

"I'm okay Mom…not really that hungry," I replied. She grunted.

"Are my babies going to be home tonight? I don't think I've seen either of them all week," she stated referring to my seventeen and eighteen-year-old children.

I chuckled, "Harrison is working, but Stacia should be home…want her to paint your nails tonight?"

I noticed that the pink polish that my daughter put on a couple of weeks ago was chipping. My mother wasn't vain, but she did like to take care of herself. Until the past year when she just couldn't get around as she used to, she visited the salon every Tuesday to have her hair done. Then, every other Wednesday, she would schedule a manicure. But disease and age had all but stripped her of the ability to do the things she once did. So, I and my daughter made sure she still felt and looked her best. Stacia would take care of her nails and

I would wash and set her hair in rollers every week. On appointment days, I made sure to have her breakfast early to give her time to apply what little makeup she still wore.

After lunch, we loaded up in the Tahoe and headed back home. I really needed to go grocery shopping, but that would need to wait until I could get her back to the house. She was pretty stubborn about trips out, especially in the winter. She thought it was too much of a hassle for me to take her inside the store with me, so she would rather wait in the car or stay home. However, staying in the car for her meant with the vehicle turned off so it would save gas. I tried to explain to her over the years that I really didn't care about saving gas if it meant she would be warm. But, if I left her there, with the heater on, even for a minute, I would return to the Tahoe shut-off.

I said she was stubborn.

I turned onto my paved drive and noticed a new, silver, Audi A4 sitting in my spot in front of the garage. I rolled my eyes thinking whoever this asshole was, probably needed to move so I could unload my mother safely and get her inside. I honked twice as I came closer then noticed the asshole was Jack.

My lucky day.

Jack exited his car, and I watched the cold February wind whip at his navy wool trench coat. He was tall and had a wider-than-average build, like someone who works out frequently. He keeps his hair cropped short and its brunette-auburn color had almost turned to full grey a few years ago. He always looks business casual, by normal standards, and rarely, if ever is unshaven.

His features resembled our mother, except for his height; he got that from our dad.

I rolled the window down as he got out of his car, "Hey, you need to move."

"Oh…I didn't know you had assigned parking here," he laughed.

"Well, *I* do…I need to be able to get Mom out and, on the porch,…hard to do that in the grass," I rolled my window up, rolled my eyes for good measure, and backed up my truck. Jack slowly moved his shiny new toy and parked it several feet from anything else.

God forbid it gets a scratch.

"Jackson got a new car it looks like," Mom stated flatly as I put my truck back in park.

"Yup," I replied shortly.

"Huh," was her response.

I lifted her out of the vehicle, rolled her up the ramp, then opened the door. Using my ass, I kept the screen open while tipping back the wheelchair slightly to lift it over the threshold. As she got inside, Mom locked the wheels and then took over in her walker. I folded the wheelchair and rolled it out of the way as Jack followed us with a bouquet of flowers.

"Hi, Mom! How was your treatment today?" he bent down and kissed her on the cheek.

She cut her eyes in my direction.

I shook my head, "No treatment today…just the fitting for the vest she'll wear."

"Oh…I thought she had her first session…that's what you said, right?" he frowned at me.

"Nope, need your listening ears, Jack…vest fitting this week, starts treatment on Monday…that's still the plan." I shook my head again.

Why do I even speak?

"Oh," he muttered, "Must have changed then..."

I sighed. Loudly. "Well, since you're here, you guys can visit while I run to the store..."

"Oh...no, I can't stay...Just wanted to bring these to Mom," Jack said, leaning down to give her another peck on the cheek.

"Well...thank you, son. They are just lovely," Mom thanked him.

I pursed my lips hard. Goddamn him. He could stay and talk to her. But this self-righteous, arrogant, worthless, *retired*, brother of mine clearly has more important places to be.

Clearly.

I sighed again, "Fine...Mom, are you good? Need to pee before I go?"

"No, honey, I'm good. Be right here when you get back...I'm going to take me a little nap," she yawned.

Perfect.

Jack walked out with me, "Are you sure it's smart to leave her all alone here? What if something happens?"

"Am I supposed to let her starve? I have to get groceries, Jack. What do you think is gonna happen? She's going to lay there and take a nap...you heard her. If you're so concerned, then stay with her until I get back," I suggested sharply.

"I have a meeting..." he began until I cut him off.

"Fine...go to your meeting...meanwhile, I'm going to the store to pick up food, shampoo, bath soap, toilet paper, and diapers for *our* mother," I replied, testily.

"What's your problem?" he countered.

I shook my head as I got into my Tahoe, "Nothing

Jack, just tired of worthless people."

Fuck off, Jack.

3

February 28

Today is the day.

The first of five treatments Mom will receive in the treatment for her lung cancer. It was a great day, the only exception was the cold, beating rain that thundered on the roof. Mom's appointment wasn't until eleven that morning, she had just finished her breakfast, and was dressing in her bedroom. I had my only cup of coffee for the day and had just finished throwing my hair into a ponytail when the doorbell rang.

"Just a min!" I called as I rushed to the door with Beegee at my heel.

It rang again and the dog barked wildly.

"Hang on just a sec..." I said angrily under my breath and opened the door wide.

"Oh, my God!" I exclaimed, "Remy! You're home!"

I threw my arms around my twin brother and hugged him tightly.

"Hey Jer…this a good time?" he asked, and I stepped to the side to let him pass. Beegee clamored for attention at his feet.

"Of course!" I was genuinely happy to see him.

We were twins, fraternal that is, even though we looked ridiculously similar with our wavy brown hair and green eyes. We spent a lot of time together as children and for obvious reasons, we were, in fact, very close. Even in middle and high school when kids had a tendency to work their way through different friends from all walks of life, Remy and I have just always been the best of friends. As an adult, it seems pretty silly to call someone your *best friend*, but that's exactly what we are. He knows all my secrets and I know his. It was Remy I talked to when Rhett and I had our first kiss and our first fight. And he knew he could lean on me when his first wife miscarried their baby and their relationship fell apart seemingly overnight.

Jeremy and Jera: two peas in a pod.

"Why didn't you tell me you were coming in today?" I asked.

"What? And give you a chance to expect me…no way!" he hugged me. "Where's Mom?"

"She's dressing…she'll be excited to see you," I said. I looked my brother over. His dark chestnut hair had gotten longer, and he had grown a beard since the last time I saw him, three months ago, but he looked well overall. I worried about him taking care of himself and being all alone on the road. When he took this job, he sold his house, and most of its contents, and paid cash for a brand new, sixteen-foot, Cherokee Wolf Pup trailer and a Ram twenty-five hundred truck. He had reduced his life to those two items, taking to traveling and working. He loves being a nomad. Mom wants him to settle down and try, again, to have a family.

"I don't think I'm the marrying kind, Mom," he told her once.

She scoffed, "Pfft. You're smart, hardworking, and handsome…any woman in their right mind would have you."

I think that was the problem with the second wife; she wasn't quite in her right mind. Unlike Remy's first wife, Katie, who was kind, sweet, and a little quiet, Stephanie was, in short, a train wreck looking for a place to happen. They met at a lake party a year after Remy and Katie's divorce was finalized. The way my brother tells it, she came up to him, very drunk, and sat in his lap. He thought she was cute, so he didn't object. But, after she vomited in the fire pit, he walked her back to her tent and thought he wouldn't see her again.

Oh, he was wrong.

She came looking for him the next morning and from then forward, they were inseparable. He proposed to her six months later and they eloped the weekend after that. It made my mom happy to see *him* happy; I, however, was skeptical. It wasn't anything overt that made me not trust her, but at first, I think I found her brashness, her loudness, and her dramatization of everything a bit much. She was a one-upper. If you had a story, she had one better.

A year into their marriage, Remy started to get suspicious that she was being unfaithful. She would go out every weekend, partying with her friends with some nights not coming home at all. He tried talking to her, reasoning with her, arguing with her, but she didn't seem to care. Then, items from their house started coming up missing; her engagement ring, an old pellet gun our dad gave him when we were children, and a tablet, to name a few. I tried to talk to Remy, but he seemed to have blinders on. I felt for my brother because I knew he was struggling to keep this marriage afloat; he didn't want to be like Jack. He wanted someone to love him.

The beginning of the end came when Remy went to use his debit card at the grocery store for milk, bread, and sandwich ham. The total came to eight dollars and thirty-two cents, but when he swiped his card, it was declined. Remy was furious at the cashier because he knew he had around fifteen-hundred dollars in his account; he had just been paid that morning. But when he called the bank to find out what the problem was, reality slammed him in the chest like a semi-truck and his world came crashing down. The agent he spoke with said his account had been overdrawn by more than two-thousand dollars before his payroll cleared. Remy's fury turned to shame as he had never in his life been in debt. Stephanie had laid the straw that broke that camel's back.

But Remy is a resilient person and he started adding up all the clues as he waited for her to come home for two days. He wanted to confront her. While he waited, he made calls to every merchant she had used and worked out deals to pay back all the money. He also called pawn shops looking for the missing items from his house; he only found one thing and with it, their destiny as a happily married couple ended.

Stephanie walked in the back door of the house early on a cloudy November Sunday to find Remy sitting on the sofa waiting for her. She tried to appease him with tales of woe; something about a lost cell phone and running out of gas, but he wasn't buying what she was trying to sell. But he also didn't want to argue with her anymore, so he took her engagement ring out of the front pocket of his jeans and showed it to her; Remy told me later she turned as white a sheet when she saw it. He had already packed her clothes and placed them on the front porch. He simply told her to get out.

She argued, cried, demanded, and lied to get to stay. She stooped so low as to tell my brother she had just miscarried *their* baby; but he remained stoic and wouldn't listen to her lies. She finally left, and Remy filed for divorce the next day. When Stephanie was served the papers, is when the real fireworks began. She falsely reported to our local police department that he had been beating her, she called his work trying to get him fired, she spread rumors around their circle of friends that he was a drug addict and had gotten her hooked on pills, and she poured an entire bag of sugar in the gas tank of his truck. But her grand finale came when Remy hired our friend, Holly, to clean his house. He was working so much overtime to pay for the bounced checks and the divorce, he barely had time to breathe, let alone, keep a house. While showing Holly around, they heard a loud BOOM! and the house shook from its foundation to roof. Remy ran out onto the front porch to find that Stephanie had run her Silverado into the side of the small brick home. After rolling out of the driver's seat, obviously high on whatever her drug of choice was, she began to threaten Holly. My brother simply shut and locked the door and called the police. The drama continued until the papers were signed, at which point, Stephanie had seemingly moved on to her next target.

Yeah, I said what I said.

"I don't think I'm the marrying kind," he said.

That comment still stabs me in the heart.

My brother and I drove our mother to the cancer center that day for her treatment. Mom knew generally what to expect beyond the heavy metal doors and she wasn't as nervous as I anticipated. But that may have been also due to her lifted spirits at Remy being home. The treatment itself took about ten minutes, but from the time we entered the door of the center until the nurse, Sarah, rolled mom out, about an hour had passed. We ate lunch and Remy sat in the truck with mom while I ran into the store to grab her more bladder leak pads.

It's a dirty business getting older.

Once home, Mom was wiped out and went to her room for a nap with Beegee not far behind. I busied myself with laundry and mopped the kitchen floor while Remy dusted the living room for me. I took the chicken out of the freezer for dinner for us, a pork chop for mom as she refuses to eat "ground buzzard" and then decided to take a small break. I plopped myself on the sofa with my Diet Coke and noticed Remy watching me.

"What, weirdo?" I took a pull off my bottle and laughed.

He narrowed his eyes at me, tilting his head, "How are *you* doing?"

"Whaddya mean?" I wrinkled my nose.

"You know…with all this? Mom…cancer…" he shook his head at me as if to say *'duh, dumbass'.*

I shrugged, "I'm fine…it is what it is."

"Fuuckk," he rolled his eyes and head back

dramatically.

"What!?" I chuckled again.

He mocked me, "*It is what it is*…bullshit! You forget we're basically the same person…so, when I ask how you are…it's like when you asked Harrison if he broke a lamp that one time with the baseball bat…I already know the answer."

He paused.

"Although I will say, you seem to be handling all this pretty well," he added.

I took another drink; I love Diet Coke.

"Well, it's true," I said, "It is what it is…I don't have time to stop and dwell on…well…anything. I'm too busy, Rem. It's like having a toddler at home again…only this time, I get to be a stay-at-home mom and I have two teenage kids…and a dog."

"And…you don't need any help?" he eyed me.

"Rhett and the kids help," I offered.

"He's a full-time teacher and coach…and the kids have their own thing," Remy threw the comment like a challenge.

I snickered, "Okay smart ass…who would you suggest? Aunt Jean? or Maybe Aunt Yvonne? Better yet…let me ask blind Aunt Patty to come help. Maybe she could drive…"

"You know what I mean," he sighed. "Just someone to come give you a break every once in a while."

I shook my head. I could be just as obstinate, hard-headed, and stubborn as our mother; more so even. She was *my* responsibility and *my* place in life right now. There was literally no one else that was better equipped to take care of her, and I would be damned if she went to a nursing home.

"Well, that's why you're here," I smiled brightly at

him. "You can hang out and watch Mom while I have some alone time."

My brother smiled at me and nodded, but I knew this conversation wasn't over. He was worried I would get burned out with this new round of health issues. Maybe he had a reason to worry, maybe not. I would ask for help when the time came and he should know that, but for now, life was good.

4

March 5

The month of March didn't start any better than February ended. The cold rain still fell from the sky and the wind was piercing and sharp. It was good to have Remy home for Mom's first week of treatments and he was a huge help; he even took her by himself on Friday to give me a break.

One would ask what I did with my time alone.

I took a long shower, washed my hair, and sat on my sofa watching daytime television garbage while savoring my daily cup of coffee.

All in my bathrobe.

I live a privileged life.

Sunday came too quickly for me though and I got a little depressed as I stirred breakfast gravy in the pot. I didn't want Remy to leave. We had had such a great week together hanging out and spending time with

Rhett and the kids; I didn't want it to end. Even Mom's mood was lifted, and her laugh was a bit louder with Remy around. He was able to see both of the kids play in their final basketball games and we spent most evenings playing cards with Mom after dinner.

"Hey…" he said hoarsely as he slinked in the back door and through the kitchen. Beegee, who sat at my feet waiting for her morning offerings, whined when he came in and he bent down to scratch her head. Remy pulled a mug out of the cupboard and poured himself a cup of dark coffee.

"Hey," I said softly as I continued stirring the thickening liquid.

He eyed me over his cup, "What's the matter?"

Pursing my lips, I shook my head.

"What?" he asked again, insistently.

"Nothing…I just…" I shrugged. "I'm gonna miss you, Rem."

He walked over and put his arm around my shoulder, "I'm just a phone call away…and I'll be back in about a month. I don't get breakfast this good on the road…this guy's gotta eat."

"You're hopeless," I rolled my eyes, laughing.

For the first time in a long time, probably since last Christmas, my whole family sat around the dining room table for breakfast. It was nice to be able to look around that block of varnished wood and see three generations of us sharing a meal. I breathed in that moment and burned it into my brain. I didn't want to ever forget what it felt like to have the aura of contentment around us in that brief period of time. I would have sat there forever and made the moment last.

5

March 31

Today started just as good as any have in the past couple of years. I was awake at five, in time to get something quick together for Rhett and the kids for breakfast. After seeing them off to school, I poured myself a cup of coffee and fried up an egg and toast for Mom's breakfast. Like every morning, Beegee was at my feet barking and begging for food. I filled her kibble bowl, but the dog looked at it and then looked back at me. It was then realized I hadn't heard anything from Mom's room all morning, so I set off to sneak a peek just to see if she had even stirred.

I opened the door and peered inside, but she wasn't in her bed. I pushed the door wide and strode in, Beegee at my heels, barking.

"Mom?" I called happily as I walked toward the bathroom. "Bee! Would you hush?"

No answer.

I pushed on the bathroom door but met resistance.

"Mom?" I called again and pushed harder on the door. When I did, a faint moan replied. Beegee, who hadn't left my side began to bark furiously. My heart raced as panic started to set in my bones. I shoved the door with my shoulder as hard as I could, making a space between it and the jamb just wide enough for me to slip through. There on the white tile lay my mother, her feet holding the door in place.

"Oh, my God! Mom!" I screamed, running to her side to check if she was conscious. "Mom!" I yelled in her face and this time her head rolled from side to side. "Don't move, Mom…I'm getting help…Beegee, stay!"

I grabbed the cordless phone from her bedside table and dialed 911. The kind operator stayed with me on the phone until the paramedics arrived five minutes later. As they worked to check her condition and get her on the gurney, I quickly found my shoes and threw my long hair into a ponytail; all of which took me only a minute and a half.

Because she couldn't answer their questions, they asked to take her to the emergency room for treatment. I, of course, agreed and followed them out while they loaded her into the ambulance. I stayed on their tail all the way through the city, to the hospital, until I was forced to park in the adjacent lot. I made it inside just as they rolled her to the admission desk.

Emergency rooms are not my friend as I find myself becoming increasingly agitated as the minutes tick by. I have so much compassion for the sick and infirm that have to spend hours upon hours waiting to be seen. Most of them are overcrowded and either too hot or too cold and the chaos of annoying alarms is enough to send a sane person mad.

Luckily, the triage nurse deemed my mother's case

as critical and we were allowed access to a room almost immediately. After being moved over to the hospital bed, the paramedics finished their paperwork quickly and left. A floor nurse entered the small space and asked for a detailed version of events. After this, another floor nurse came in and again asked for a reason for the visit. By this time, Mom was starting to come around a little but was very agitated. They suggested restraints.

"Absolutely not!" I ordered.

"Ma'am…she and our staff need to be safe," the tall blonde nurse with razor-sharp features looked at me over her glasses. "It's policy."

"How about she's scared and doesn't know where she is or why!?" I snapped back and then leaned in so my mother could see my face. "Hey Mama…it's okay…"

I stroked her hair.

"It's going to be okay…you're in the hospital…"

She gave me a confused look.

"You were on the floor in the bathroom…can you talk to me? Can you tell me what happened?" I said more calmly than I felt.

Her voice was hoarse, "No…"

"It's okay Mom…there are a couple nurses here that are going to *help*," I cut my eyes at the tall woman with the glasses. "They need to run an IV and give you fluids, okay?"

My mother nodded, relaxing.

I brought my chair closer with my toe, so I didn't have to release my mother's hand as I sat next to her bed. I pursed my lips at the nurse and eyed her. She and her counterpart began working again in silence. I sat holding my mother's hand for a bit longer when the doctor made an appearance.

He reached over my mom and shook my hand introducing himself, "Good morning…I'm Dr. Anthony Blake…I hear we've taken quite the tumble today, Ms. Evelyn."

After his cursory exam, he ordered more blood tests than I think it took to diagnose her Multiple Sclerosis, x-rays, and a CAT scan. He was nothing if not thorough.

After she returned from the X-ray and left for her scan, I realized I hadn't called anyone to tell them what had happened and by this time, we had been there for hours. The thought of making a dozen phone calls felt overwhelming, so I started with the easiest, Rhett, then ended with the person who I knew would make a difficult situation even harder, my dear brother Jack. By the time everyone arrived at the hospital, the staff was finally moving mom to a room on the third floor.

Rhett, our children, Jack and his wife Elaine, and I stood in the waiting room for her to arrive on the floor.

"What happened?" Jack demanded.

"Doctor thinks it was a stroke…" I attempted to explain.

"The cancer?" he interrupted.

I'm sure my face was one of pure confusion at his comment as he looked at me like I was an idiot.

"The cancer, Jera…is it because it's spreading? She needs to have the chemo…" he snapped at me.

I shook my head, "No…no Jack. If you want to blame something, then blame the MS…it makes her more susceptible to them…" I said as calmly as possible.

"They need to speak with her oncologist," he replied.

"Neurologist," I corrected.

He glared at me, "I said what I said…her *oncologist* needs to be informed. I want her checked again…"

I rolled my eyes.

"You have something to say, Jera?" he snapped, his tone hateful and a flash of memory hit me like a hammer.

***

It was summer and as typical for Missouri, the late morning air was already thick and humid. Remy and I were up early to ride our bikes through the neighborhood, but now, it was getting almost too hot to breathe. We decided that we probably should get back to the house before Jack was awake anyway or we knew he'd leave and probably lock us out.

We threw our bikes on the ground next to the front door and went inside. The screen made a familiar crashing sound behind us as it slammed shut. I was so thirsty after all the play, so I grabbed a glass of red Kool-Aid out of the refrigerator.

"Jera!" Remy yelled from the hallway.

I gulped my drink, "What!?" I heard my brother's quick footsteps coming toward the kitchen.

"Uhmm…you better come look," Remy's face looked fearful, and I was confused. I sat my empty glass on the counter and followed him back to my room.

It was utterly destroyed.

When I say 'utterly destroyed' what I mean is that while I was a ten-year-old child who did not keep the tidiest of spaces, this looked as though a tornado had run a path in my room. It was definitely not how I left it this earlier this morning. It suddenly hit me that I had been playing with my set of miniature ceramic dolls I had received for Christmas. I left them lined up on my bedspread when I left.

Panic set in.

I started digging frantically through the rumpled mess of sheets and blankets from my now-stripped bed. One. Two. Three. I found three of them…

Where was the fourth? Where was the redhead with soft alabaster skin who wore the tiny satin dress? Tears started forming in my eyes and Remy began helping me search.

"Uh oh," he said as he pulled a tiny arm from under a pillowcase.

"No!" I cried as I snatched the arm from his hand. The tears fell faster, and Remy looked harder for the rest of her. It only took him a few more moments to find her twisted body. He handed her to me delicately.

"I'm sorry, Jera," he whispered. "What happened in here anyway?"

I shook my head, "I don't know."

"I do," Jack's voice bellowed from my doorway. "Dad told you to make your bed…you didn't…so now you have to."

"You aren't dad, Jack," Remy growled.

"Shut up, punkass!" Jack snarled, shoving Remy.

"You broke my doll!" I yelled.

"So? Too bad…should have done what dad told you to do," Jack smirked.

"Mom will make you buy her another one," Remy charged on. Jack pulled back his fist, acting like he would punch Remy.

I was so angry at Jack. He had no right to come into my room and he had no right to touch my things. I glared at my brother and swore I would never forgive him.

He only smirked more, "What? You got something to say, midget?"

***

I took a deep breath…I had had enough of him already. But, before I could speak, Rhett stepped between us. He held my shoulders then glanced back at my older brother, "Enough, Jack."

Jack turned in a huff as he and Elaine strode toward the nurse's station.

Rhett's eyes moved over and saw through me; he could always do that. He knew what I was thinking before I could even know myself and he had an uncanny ability to anticipate my every move. I've always teased he was a witch in a former life; he maintains it's the years of military training. However he does it, it always makes me feel safe.

We met in high school at Courtwarming, my sophomore year. He was tall, strongly built with sandy hair, piercing blue eyes, and a Senior. He asked me, very politely, if I cared to dance. At the time, I was doing a very impressive job holding up the wall, so of course, I accepted. He admitted to me, years later, that it had taken him most of that school year to work up the courage to ask for that dance. I never would have believed him at the time as he was and has always been the epitome of confidence.

After that night, we spent nearly as much time together as Remy and me. So much so that even he and Remy were nearly inseparable, but that was almost to be expected since Rhett had no siblings of his own. Jack and Rhett were different, to say the least. My eldest brother did his best to intimidate Rhett from the word go; something that he completely ignored. This only irritated Jack further because he "had to protect his little sister," or whatever his bullshit drivel was at the time. But the more Jack rallied against our relationship, the more our Mom and Dad seemed to like it. They thought my boyfriend, Rhett, was an ace. After his high school graduation three months later, Rhett joined the Marine Corps and was shipped out to Camp Pendleton, in California, for boot camp. Jack was arrogantly ecstatic and started planting ideas in my head as soon as the bus left.

It was a very long summer that year.

Rhett came home for almost two weeks after boot camp before heading off to military police training. By this time, I was convinced that he would want to break off our relationship, I mean, I wasn't quite seventeen when he came home. A boy left and a man returned…what did he want with this *girl*? To my relief and my brother's utter irritation, Rhett was just as overjoyed and excited to see me as I was him. Two other things happened when he came back. The first was Jack's reaction to Rhett's physical transformation that had taken place while he was away. It seemed the *intimidator* had become the *imtidate-ee* and Jack started keeping his comments about our relationship to himself. Second, right before he left again, Rhett asked me to marry him.

Now, before anyone loses their mind, let me explain.

Were we too young? Yes, absolutely. Did we *get* married immediately? Oh, hell no. C'mon…I was seventeen, and *that* would have been crazy. What we did was commit ourselves to each other and set our future in motion. Something to this day I don't regret for a second.

I graduated high school and made it through two years of college before we actually took the trip down the aisle; I was twenty, and he was twenty-three. To this day, I still think our wedding photo is the most beautiful picture in the world; I've always loved seeing Rhett in his dress uniform. After our very short honeymoon, we moved to Oceanside for a year, then Virginia for another year. It was an exciting time for the both of us, but we soon realized that my moving around wasn't going to fit in with our long-term goals. When he received his first orders to go overseas, we decided that it would be best if I moved back to the home state where I could finish school and he would visit when he could. I waited and worried while he was stationed in Cuba, Japan, and finally back stateside in Texas. After twelve years of service, Rhett decided it was time for other goals to be conquered so he left the Corps, came home, and started college.

We lived a very simple life in those first years after he left the Marines. We did our best to live below our means and save every penny we could. I worked in the local high school, and he took a weekend job in the sheriff's department as a deputy; two of the most underpaid professions, in my opinion. He always enjoyed law enforcement, but he really wanted to reach kids before they made the mistakes that set them on the wrong path, so he became a teacher also. It was during his third semester at university that we found out we were expecting our son, Harrison. We had him in January of the following year and by July of the same year, we were pregnant with Stacia.

We were older now and wiser. Rhett's hair was starting to gray around the temples and his face was a little more handsomely aged, but his eyes were still sharply blue as they stared at me. He gave me a familiar look that said, *'Let me fix it'*. But he couldn't. I gave him my own familiar look back and he immediately wrapped his strong arms around me. I sobbed into my husband's chest without realizing at the moment the repercussions of that act; Rhett wouldn't forget who made me cry and why.

"Shhhh," he comforted me in my ear.

"I don't know how much more I can take, Rhett," I whispered.

"No more…you're done with this," his voice was almost commanding.

I pulled away, looked into his eyes, and sighed, "It's not worth the fight."

His head pulled slightly to the right, and he gave me a side-eye.

I knew what he was saying. He didn't believe me for a second; I've always been a fighter. But the constant arguments with Jack about our mother's care were beginning to be more than I could take, especially at this moment.

"She's not quite ready," Elaine stated softly as the couple made their way back into the waiting room.

"Jera," Jack began, and Rhett gave him a look of warning. Jack swallowed hard, and softened his voice, but not its tone, "Maybe it's time for Mom to go somewhere she can be…"

I looked up at my brother and dared him to finish the sentence.

"Mom is perfectly cared for in *my* home. She has one on one attention and four people who are always at her beck and call…she will get no better care anywhere else. Unless you would like her to move in with you?"

Fuck off, Jack.

6

April 5

The stroke my mother had left her with damaged vocal cords that caused her voice to sound very hoarse. I started to tease her that she was now as sexy as Kathleen Turner, which made her laugh. The hospital had deemed her a fall risk, so while she was there, they didn't allow her to move about as freely as she would have at home. Because of the lack of normal movement combined with the stroke damage, it was determined she would need in-house rehabilitation for three weeks. One of my two worst fears was coming to fruition: My mother was going into a nursing home.

I was petrified.

Some may ask why? Why would I be so concerned with a temporary stay at a place that should be more than qualified to care for an eighty-ish-year-old woman with multiple sclerosis, chronic obstructive pulmonary disease, and lung cancer? Well, I have my reasons.

Primarily of which is, I worked as a Certified

Nursing Assistant while in college. And while I found the work extremely difficult at times, it was amazingly rewarding. And while most of my co-workers were very kind-hearted and cared deeply for our residents, there were those that were there only for a paycheck. So, when you combine the physically and mentally demanding workload with a low wage, it will, at times, spell disaster. And speaking of the pay, this is another profession that is overwhelmingly underpaid, and sometimes, you get what you pay for.

I watched, brokenhearted, as they loaded my mother into another ambulance to escort her to Greenlawn Residential Care and Rehabilitation. Luckily, it was only an eight-minute drive from my house so, in the worst-case scenario, I could be there quickly. I again followed the rig through the city and onto the curved blacktop driveway of the center. It was beautiful enough on the outside, with its plush green grass and magazine-worthy landscaping; but I could already smell the odor of disinfectant in my nose. They unloaded my mother, and we waited as a short, gray-haired nurse escorted us to where she would be staying; room 105. The pair of paramedics were very sweet as they handled my mom and maneuvered her into a manual lift bed that looked as though it came directly out of the 1970s. She smiled at them as they raised the head of the bed, placing her in a more seated position. The mousy-gray-haired nurse checked mom in, took her vitals, and allowed her to peruse a menu so she could tell them her preferences, all while taking inventory of her medication.

That first night was so hard to walk away from. When she was in the hospital, I knew it was temporary, but this felt like I was abandoning her. It broke my heart even though my brain kept telling me I would see her tomorrow… the next day, and the next. She wouldn't go a day without seeing me and I prayed that the three weeks would fly past. She never wavered, she never gave me a guilty look, but I felt it inside. I felt like I had failed her in some way when logically, I hadn't. Rhett and I were so blessed to have healthy children because I could only imagine that this is what it felt like to leave your child in the care of strangers. She would only be here for a short time…I would make sure of it; even if she wasn't one hundred percent at the end of the twenty-one days, I would bring my mother home.

7

April 16

"How's she doing?" Remy asked.

I sighed. I missed her so much.

"She's good…made friends with her roommate. They race each other to the dining room every night at dinner," I forced my voice to sound light.

He paused. It had been eleven days since my mother had been sent to Greenlawn Residential Care for physical therapy after her stroke. Remy called every evening around seven to check on her day and to chat. He had not been able to make it home quite yet, but he made sure he called. I think he feels like I'm lost.

I am.

"So," I hear him take a pull of his beer, "You gonna tell me the same bullshit story you've told me for two weeks now about how *you're* handling this or are you ready to live in reality?"

I frowned, "What are you talking about?"

"Jer, we've had nearly the same conversation every

single night…I ask about mom, then I ask about you…you lie to me, then I talk to Rhett," he responded matter-of-factly.

"What do you mean, you talk to Rhett?" I snapped.

"Look, if you're not gonna tell me what's going on with you, I'll get the information another way."

He seemed unbothered by my change in attitude.

"Not sure I like my brother and my husband talking about me behind my back," I remarked as I rounded the corner of the hallway and stared at Rhett sitting on the sofa with our son.

Remy's voice softened, "Jer…I'm just worried about you, that's all. I know this has to be harder on you than anyone…just stop trying to put on the *Jera the brave'* face with me…I see through it."

I hated it when he was right. I've never wanted to put anyone out on my account. I've always been independent and relatively self-sufficient. I'm a by-product of parents that had their own careers, brothers that hated each other, and the United States military. I am the epitome of a Gen-Xer.

That did *not* mean my twin got to call me out though; but this time, I'd allow it.

"Sorry Rem," I apologized. "You're right…I'm tired of worrying about what's going on when I'm not there…I just want her home so bad."

Hot tears formed in my eyes, and I looked skyward as I willed them away.

"I'll be okay…just ten more days, right?" I said.

I could hear the smile in my brother's voice, "That's right…ten days."

After a few more minutes, I ended my phone call with Remy. Ten days wouldn't be so bad, right? I mean, I'd made it this far. It was just difficult not really knowing what to do with myself. The past few years, mom and I had developed quite a routine. I got to the point where I could anticipate every need she had. It was just life. Now, with her out of the house, my days were unbalanced, and I had to quickly develop new routines.

Would this be what it was like when she passed away?

I didn't want to imagine my life without her, but I also had to live in the here and now. She *was* in her eighties. She *did* have major health issues before the cancer. What would I do with myself after that time came? Maybe I would go back to teaching; it was my first love. Or maybe I would go back to school and continue my own education. Rhett would be ready for retirement in the next several years, we could always travel. The maybes and what-ifs compounded my brain until I fell onto my side of the bed and passed out of exhaustion. It felt like just moments later when the other side of the bed was depressed as Rhett laid down for the night. I rolled on my side and faced him.

"Goodnight," I said sleepily.

I could feel his eyes staring at me in the dim light, but I never moved. He brushed loose strands of hair from my face as I felt his eyes continue to watch me.

"Did you eat tonight?" he asked aloud.

He knew I wasn't sleeping. Sometimes, his ability as an all-knowing human can be annoying. But honestly, it didn't take much to annoy me these days.

I opened my eyes slowly, "I don't remember."

"Damn it, Jera," he sighed heavily.

"Rhett, don't start," I was exhausted and didn't want to hear what he was going to say because I knew he would be right, and under normal circumstances, I would agree with him. My priorities were skewed at the moment, and I've put myself last on the list. We had been together nearly thirty years; this shouldn't really be a surprise to him. I looked him dead in the face as he watched me, cocking an eyebrow.

I know it's wrong, especially at this moment, but damn…this man is sexy, even when he's irritated at me.

"What?" I asked.

It was then he raised both brows at me; he had a way of speaking without words.

"What!?" I demanded again.

"Breakfast," he frowned.

"Toast with peanut butter…coffee," I replied.

"Lunch," he tilted his head.

That I had to think about. I knew I was at the home with Mom, but did I eat?

"Handful of chips…I think. Diet Coke," I was honestly trying to remember.

Rhett stared at me flatly, "Dinner."

I was so busted.

"Couple of Harry's fries," I said softly.

He gave me a *'see my point?'* look.

"I'm sorry," I whispered.

His face softened, "Don't you ever apologize…But, Jer, I'm worried about you. You can't take care of your mom if you don't take care of yourself. Diet Coke and a handful of chips aren't going to keep you going. What happens if you get sick…you gonna leave everything for Jack to do?"

Ouch. That hit hard.

"Well?" he asked as a sly smile spread across his

ridiculously handsome face.

I smiled back, rolled out of bed, and went to the kitchen to fix a sandwich. I assumed when I returned, he would be asleep, but to my delight, he wasn't. He sat leaning against the headboard, his reading glasses sitting on the bridge of his strong nose, looking at a book. I plopped next to him and watched. A realization that I was naturally aware of already, graced my mind: This man was my rock. I wouldn't have made it this far without him. Thinking those thoughts doesn't diminish my own accomplishments, I'm just grateful that he's been along for the ride.

8

April 17

The smell of floor disinfectant and surface sanitizer assaulted my nostrils as I opened the second set of glass security doors to the nursing home. Smiling at the nurse at the front desk, I made an immediate right turn down my mother's hallway. I expected to find her room empty and to wait for her to come back from her morning therapy, but what I found surprised me a little. The room was about ten degrees too warm, and it felt like I ran into a hot, humid, and invisible wall as I entered. Mom laid on her back, blankets pulled to her chin, sleeping. I called to her as I approached.

"Mom?" I leaned down where I knew she could hear me.

She didn't move.

"Mom?" I shouted a little louder and reached for her shoulder; it was cold and clammy. I stripped the blankets from her and took her hands which felt the same as the rest of her body.

"Mom! Can you hear me? I need you to open your eyes," I was practically yelling in her face now, but I finally did get a response as her eyes attempted to flutter open.

"So…cold…" her rough voice said weakly. I pushed the call button that was clipped to her nightgown. In what felt like several minutes, the speaker on the wall crackled and a voice responded.

"Can I help you?"

"Yes, we need a nurse in here…now!" I yelled.

"What's the problem, ma'am?" the voice asked.

I was becoming very impatient and didn't want to deal with whatever bullshit this person was getting ready to dish out. I stood out in the hall and yelled out, "Just get a nurse in here!"

Within a minute, a dark-haired woman, dressed in white scrubs, came strolling quickly into the room. "What's going on?" she asked. "Good lord! Why is it so hot in here?"

"I found her like this…heater turned up…covers to her chin…she cold and clammy and non-responsive. How long has she been like this?" I demanded.

The middle-aged woman shook her head, "I have no idea, it's not my hall today." She got close to mom's face, "Miss Evelyn. Miss Evelyn…can you hear me?"

Mom's eyes fluttered, but she never spoke.

The nurse reached into her jacket and pulled out a blood pressure cuff, wrapping it around my mother's arm. She pumped the bulb to add air to the bladder and placed the end of the stethoscope in the crook of Mom's arm. As she released the air, I watched the look of confusion and then concern drape over the nurse's face.

"What is it?" I asked as she pulled the Velcro off

the cuff.

"It's low…eighty over sixty. I think she needs to be seen at the hospital…I'm going to send in an aide to wait with you until they arrive," she was already out of the door as she finished her sentence.

Holy. Shit.

Adrenaline flooded my body as my mind began to race thinking about what this new health issue could be. Exactly how much more could Mom deal with?

The ambulance was on site within a few minutes, and they quickly placed Mom onto the gurney and loaded her inside the unit. I, for the third time in less than a month, followed the lumbering truck through the city. This time I was smarter about my phone calls, and I decided I would talk to no one until I knew exactly what was going on and if they would keep her or not.

It took the hospital staff four hours of testing to finally come up with a diagnosis. By this time, I had drunk my fill of half-brewed coffee that had sat in the pot for six hours too long and was, as one could imagine, at the short end of my nerves when the doctor finally walked into her small exam room. Luckily, it was the same man that had treated her just a couple of weeks ago.

"Ms. McKay, I'm so sorry you've had to wait so long…but I think we know what's going on with your mom," he smiled sincerely.

I nodded, "Okay…what is it?"

"After reviewing the medication list from Greenlawn, it looks like Dr. Tuffner, changed the blood thinner she was on from warfarin to rivaroxaban. It looks like the rivaroxaban has caused some internal bleeding…we're going to need to keep her for a few days to treat the bleeding and get her rebalanced," he explained.

"Who is Dr. Tuffner? She doesn't have a doctor by that name," I politely demanded.

Dr. Blake frowned, "Oh…well, looks like he's the supervising physician for Greenlawn."

"Why? Why would he change that?" fire began to rise in my stomach. I needed to maintain my cool.

"I don't know…has she had a level check since she was discharged?" he shook his head.

"No, she hasn't. She wasn't scheduled for labs until after I brought her home," I explained.

Dr. Blake pursed his lips together in thought, "I'm not sure what I can tell you…but, not to worry…we'll get her feeling better in a few days so she can get back to therapy."

He turned on his heel and left the room.

I made sure mom was comfortable in her room before I found a quiet corner in the waiting room to call the family. Rhett was home by the time I called and told me he would be on his way. When I called Jack, I got no answer. He probably thought he was punishing me for something by not answering, but it was actually a relief. I called the house and spoke to Elaine, explaining what was happening. Elaine, who was always kind and spoke with a soft voice, the kind that could soothe even the crankiest of animals, said she would let my brother know as soon as possible. Then I called Remy and left a message.

As I waited for Rhett to arrive, thoughts of the day tumbled around in my head. Why would the physician for the nursing home take it upon himself to change my mother's medication? And why would he do it without the proper testing? I was no physician, but it made sense to check first and make sure the first medicine wasn't working before changing to a different one. Why had no one informed us of the change? All questions I would get answers to when or *if* my mother returned to therapy.

I was happy with *if*.

$$9$$

April 23

The shelves in the office of Dr. Able Tuffner were filled to the brim with books, binders, and various paperwork. The oversized oak desk that had to have been built inside the room, was home to a sleek-looking laptop and several pens. His large leather, wing-back desk chair sat empty as I waited. I hated waiting on people. I'm a person who is *usually* on time and find being late a sign of disrespect. Is that to say I've never been late a day in my life? No, not at all. Everybody has run five or even ten minutes behind and been in a situation where you apologize all over yourself, thanking the other party for waiting. But Dr. Tuffner was working on more than twenty-five minutes. His conversation, which I could hear through the paper-thin walls of the rehab's office area, had less to do with the care of a resident and more to do with the size of the trout he caught the weekend before.

The longer I sat, the more I quietly seethed.

I finally heard the neighboring door shut and his door almost immediately opened. He squeezed around the corner of his desk and faced me.

"Ms. McKay, I'm sorry to keep you waiting," his grey eyes looked at me over half-moon glasses.

I did my best to be pleasant, "Thank you for seeing me."

"Of course…I hear you have a question about the care of Mrs. Evelyn Northland?" he flipped through a folder he had carried into the room. "Can I ask how you are related to Mrs. Northland?"

"I'm her daughter and primary caregiver," I responded and felt a little more irritated. Shouldn't this be in the chart he was holding?

"Ah…yes…I see. So, what questions do you have?" he placed the open folder on the desk and propped his elbows on it.

"Well, I'm wondering why you changed her medication…after her stroke, her hospitalist and neurologist placed her on Warfarin for blood clots…you changed it. Why?" I asked.

He gave me an audacious look as if I had just challenged his manhood.

"Because I did," he said sharply.

I smiled sweetly, "Yes, I'm aware you *did*…I'm asking *why*."

"I don't have time to explain chemistry or medical science to you, Miss. Just be assured that I thought it was the best course of action," his voice haughty.

My patience was now out. I've never been someone to be outwardly or purposefully rude, but I would be damned if this quack was going to talk down to me.

"You are not her physician, *sir*. You don't get to make those decisions without consulting, at the very least, her neurologist…" I charged.

"I don't need to consult for anyone that is under my care!" he loudly interrupted.

"Sir, you will not talk over me!" My voice now was starting to rise in volume. "I am not some pathetic family member who dropped off their parents, never to be heard from again! You will talk to me with respect."

"Young lady…you won't speak to me like that! These residents see *me*…I have the ultimate say in their care!" he stood from his chair and practically yelled in my face.

"The hell you do! And do *not* call me young lady. You're mistake nearly killed my mother…I *will* remove her from your care," I roared, rising from my seat.

A small group of staff began to gather outside the open door.

"You listen to me," his voice dropped to a near-dangerous level, "If you attempt to remove your mother from this facility, I *will* call the state and report you for abuse."

I narrowed my eyes at him and met his tone, "You call the state. Call the governor. I don't give a damn who you call…But, according to that very large sign that hangs in the hallway behind me, my mother has the right to informed consent, treatment choice, and even the refusal of treatment. Maybe you're the one that needs some… *education*. Now, since I am my mother's health proxy, you are no longer allowed to treat her… I'll schedule and provide transportation to any appointments she needs from here on out until the end of her therapy. Are *we* clear?"

My face dared him to disagree with me. It was at that moment a short, round woman with bright red hair and heavy makeup poked her head inside the threshold.

"Dr. Tuffner, everything alright?" her eyes cut between the pair of us. I continued to stare him down before turning toward the woman.

"I need a document revoking Dr. Tuffner's ability to treat my mother…and don't worry, she'll sign it herself," I added sharply. The woman looked from the glaring doctor and then back to me again.

"I'll get the social worker," she whispered as she turned to leave.

Dr. Tuffner's jaw clenched, "You can't do that."

My head snapped back to him. "Watch me. I'm not a litigious person, *Mr.* Tuffner," I'll also be damned if I was going to give this man any more respect, "But if I find out you so much as step foot in my mother's room, we'll find out how good your malpractice insurance really is."

I turned on my heel and stormed from the room.

10

April 30

It had been a week since my run-in with Dr. Tuffner over what I deemed was the gross malpractice treatment of my mother. He continued to avoid me at every turn, even going so far as to remove himself from the dining room one evening while I sat visiting with my mother and her table mates. It was probably a smart move on his part, as I didn't want to be in the same room as him and was still pissed off. His avoidance of me only bolstered my belief that he was an idiot.

Today was a special day and I wasn't going to allow my feelings for Dr. Twit to ruin it for me or mom; Remy had finally made it back home.

I didn't tell our mother he was coming with me that day, or that the kids were out of school, and they too would be in tow. So, when this rag-tag group sauntered into her room with flowers, balloons, and fast-food take-out for a picnic outside, it was pure joy as her face lit the room.

"What are all of you doing here?" she said in amazement. Her voice was sounding more normal every day.

"We thought we would surprise you, Grandma," Stacia replied as she leaned over to kiss Mom on the cheek.

She patted my daughter's face, "Thank you, sweet girl."

"Let's go outside in the sun, Grandma," Harrison smiled handsomely at her as he took control of her wheelchair. He rolled her down the long hallways and out the double doors that led to a beautifully manicured courtyard with spring flowers in full bloom. Mom pointed to a table at the far end of the sidewalk that had the most sunlight. Stacia found her grandmother's food and set it up at the end of the table. Both kids took a position to sit closest to their grandma and passed out the rest of the bags.

"Jeremy, how long have you been home?" Mom asked.

He chuckled, "I just got in last night, Mom."

"How long you gonna be home this time?" She took a bite of her cheeseburger.

"About ten days…then headed out to New Mexico for a few weeks. I'll come back through when I head to Alabama at the end of May," he grinned.

"Oh…well…Alabama. That's not too far, is it?" Mom smiled at me.

I returned her grin. Remy was never more than a straight twelve or fifteen-hour drive west or east of home, but for some reason, Mom always thought he was closer when he traveled east.

"How is my baby? How is Beegee?" she asked.

"She's fine Grandma," Stacia smiled.

"Are you ready to come home, Grandma?" Harrison asked. Mom gave him a confused look as she sipped her Diet Dr. Pepper.

"I think it will be a little while, Harry," she said through a soft smile. Both of my children grinned impishly at her, then cut their eyes in my direction. She followed suit and stared at me. No longer able to control my serious expression, I broke into laughter.

"Actually Mom," I giggled, "They're releasing you tomorrow."

I will never forget, as long as I live and breathe, the look on her softly wrinkled face. I often liken it to how a prison inmate must react when told that they will be released after a long, arduous sentence. Her eyes became crystal orbs of light, and her enormous smile was automatic and effortless.

"Tomorrow? Really?" she asked with a bit of childish wonderment that saddened me for a moment. Was her time here really that bad? Had I made the right decision when I put her here? Those thoughts I had to shake away quickly because I didn't want her happiness to waver.

"Yes, Mom, really…Dr. Brett has already signed off, as well as the physical therapist here. They are setting up continued therapy at the house three times a week, starting next week…otherwise, you're out of here," I laughed.

"Well," Mom started to say, and I noticed the small wisps of wetness beginning in her eyes, "That's just wonderful, isn't it?"

"Well, one thing, Grandma," Harrison snickered.

"What's that?"

"You'll have to kick Stacia out of your room…she's been sleeping in there with Beegee," he chuckled.

My mom turned to my daughter, smiling.

"You're such a snitch!" Stacia threw a French fry at her brother.

Mom laughed and wrapped her fingers around Stacia's hand, "That's okay sweetheart, you can share a room with Grandma, if you want."

"Alright, children," I teased loudly, "Let's get all of this cleaned up and get Grandma back inside…I'd hate for her to catch a cold in this breeze and for all our plans to be thrown out the window."

Harrison and my brother gathered all of our trash as Stacia guided her grandmother's chair back through the facility doors. By the time we got her settled back in the room, she was ready to rest for a while, so we called an aide to help her to bed for a nap before her therapy session that afternoon. I remember the lightness I felt as I left the building that day; in twenty-four hours, Mom would be home, where she belonged, and life could finally resume its normality.

11

May 12

Mother's Day

The group of people that exited that large vehicle were not the normal rag-tag bunch of fellows that usually fell out its doors. Everyone was clean, shaven, tidy, and dressed in what would be considered their Sunday best. For my group to look this put together—at the same time—was so far out of the realm of commonplace that it was nearly comical. But I was proud; this would be a day of celebration, food, and family.

Rhett had made a reservation at Savannah Tavern for their annual Mother's Day Brunch. Savannah's was an upscale restaurant located in the higher-end Wyldwood neighborhood on the south side of the city and one of my favorite places to enjoy a meal. Its decor is adventurous and airy with its high vaulted ceilings of rich timbers that are lined with tiny white LED lights. Faux animal hides hang from the walls alongside real mountings of various types of antlers and old black-and-white photographs of vast landscapes from around the world. That day, the dark wood tables that sat in neat rows throughout the open space were covered with sharp, white tablecloths and settings of shiny silverware glistening in the filtered rays of morning sun that cascaded through the enormous hardwood framed windows.

After the Matre'd checked us in, we made our way to a large table that had been made from several smaller ones pushed together. While the size of the table looked a little out of place, it was no less elegant as it had been covered with one tablecloth that fit perfectly and three round bouquets of pink and green flowers had been set along its center. My breath caught in my throat as Rhett touched the small of my back as I took in the scene.

"Happy Mother's Day," he whispered in my ear, kissing the side of my head.

I turned on tip toe and returned a peck to his cheek, "It's perfect…Thank you." I saw him shrug a little with his cute side smile.

This guy. After all these years he can still give me all the feelings with a look.

Harrison wheeled Mom next to me, "Where's Grandma sitting?"

"Well, Harry," Rhett suggested, "Since she is elder woman of honor, why don't you ask her?" Harrison instantly understood his dad's meaning and leaned down to have a conversation with his grandmother. It was decided that she would sit at the head of the table with her grandchildren on either side.

Within just a few minutes the rest of our party arrived and took their seats. Rhett and the kids had outdone themselves this year as most of our family gathered at the enormous table. Rhett's parents, Richard and Mary sat on either side of our kids and chatted with my mom. My father's brother, Chuck, and his wife, Leann were present as was my Aunt Jean, my dad's oldest sister. Remy sat on my right, across from Uncle Chuck and Jack took a position at the end of the table, opposite our mother with Elaine. I did my best to make a pleasant conversation with him.

"The kids couldn't come?" I asked, wondering about my nephews and niece. All of his children were grown and on their own now, the eldest with a small family of his own. But, I thought the question still needed to be asked.

Jack smiled slightly, "No, JJ and Anna went to her mother's…he said they and Val were going to see Kathleen later…Beckett is still at school…I'm sure he'll call Angela at some point."

Honestly, I'm not sure what I expected; Jack junior, or "JJ" was almost as arrogant and money-eyed as his father. He was a nice enough kid to us, but I wasn't really surprised that neither he nor his wife would go out of their way to visit. I honestly hadn't seen Valentine since she graduated from high school six years ago. All of the kids were products of their wealthy and overprivileged environments. Their half-brother, Beckett was at least a little more down to earth, something I was convinced he got from his mother, Jack's ex-wife number two. But Valentine and Beckett were also not as self-serving as their older brother and did at least call their grandmother from time to time just to say hello.

I felt Remy's arm around my shoulder and his hand pat me twice. More sign language. Even though he had been talking with Uncle Chuck, he heard Jack's response to my question and instinctively knew what I was thinking. I gave him a very nonchalant hug back and said to Jack, "Oh, well, that's too bad."

Savannah's has a tradition every Mother's day of bringing every woman of childbearing age a red rose and a glass of champagne at the end of the meal. Our waiter, a young dark-haired boy by the name of Jesse, carried over a tray of full glasses and began to pass them out to each woman at our table along with a beautiful flower that looked as soft as velvet. Mom giggled as she lifted the glass of bubbling liquid to her lips and took a sip.

I could feel Jack's eyes boring into me.

I lifted my own glass and sipped the sparkling wine carefully because what I really wanted was to down it like a shot. I would actively ignore him.

He leaned in, "Don't you think you should stop her?"

Damn. That didn't work.

"Stop her?" I asked, sighing deeply.

"How is that going to mix with her meds, Jer?" He eyed our mother down the table.

I felt Remy tense beside me.

"She's fine Jack…it's one tiny glass of champagne. I promise it won't hurt her," I replied. At that moment, I heard our mother gasp and begin to cough. I started to jump from my seat when Remy's hand pushed on my shoulder hard as he went in to help. Stacia was already patting her grandmother's back as Harrison handed her a goblet of water.

"Hey Mom, you alright?" Remy knelt beside her.

Her eyes widened a little as she tried to pull in a breath. "It's okay…deep breath…those bubbles will get you every time. Looks like you're out of practice with the good stuff."

This made mom grin as her coughing fit began to recede. After a few seconds, Stacia unlocked the wheels of her chair and looked over at me.

"Bathroom," she mouthed.

I stood to go with her, but Stacia shook her head, "I got it, Mom."

I sat down.

"Poor thing…getting all choked up like that," Aunt Jean remarked as her boney fingers played with the stem of her glass. "How is she really doing, hon?"

I smiled, "She's good, really…happy to be home. She's getting around the house really well with her walker…we're only using the wheelchair when we're out."

Aunt Jean shook her head, "I just worry about her…those doctors don't always tell you everything."

I frowned. Which didn't go unnoticed or unacknowledged by Aunt Jean.

"Well, they don't. Especially those foreign ones…they lie the most," she pointed one of those bony fingers at me.

The table got quiet for a moment, and I thought there was a spotlight on me. She was joking, right?

"I'm not sure what you mean," I replied.

"Foreigners honey," she stated firmly. "I mean, what kind of name is M-baye? She needs an American one…"

My eyes got wide, and I looked around the table to see if anyone else was hearing what I was. There is a southern colloquialism I learned while Rhett and I lived in Virginia years ago that I feel is appropriate in this scenario: Aunt Jean's words went over like a fart in church.

"Senegalese," I replied.

She batted her eyes at me, "Excuse me?"

"His name…Dr. Mbaye is from Senegal…received his education at Duke University, then medical school at Wash U in St. Louis…residency at Barnes," I clarified. What I wanted to say had more to do with her being a nasty bigot in her old age, but this would do.

Remy chuckled to himself as was his nature in a tense situation, especially one that his own dark humor found amusing. Aunt Jean, however, took this to mean he agreed with her.

"See Jera, even your brother knows," she grinned broadly at my twin, but apparently, Uncle Chuck had heard enough.

"Oh, dry it up Jeanie…you know that's nonsense. Christ, if we were deciding who's American by their name, then you would have been kicked out a long time ago," my uncle scolded her.

It was true…my Aunt Jean Gonzales. Her husband, my late Uncle Pete was the first in his family to be born in the United States.

She was still glaring at her brother when Stacia rolled Mom back to her spot at the table. "What did I miss?" she asked brightly.

I heard Harrison whisper something under his breath, his sister's eyes widened, and Aunt Leann snorted a short, disguised chuckle.

I'd find out about that later.

I grinned back at my mother, "Nothing at all…you better?"

My mother cut her eyes in Aunt Jean's direction

then quickly back to me, "Oh, honey, I'm fine…now…where is that handsome young man with some coffee?"

***

I placed the two small bundles of flowers in matching round globe vases and sat them on the dining room table. Stacia had helped Mom out of her wheelchair and into bed for a nap shortly after we returned from brunch. The coughing fit had exhausted her more than she wanted to admit, but when my daughter had suggested that maybe a nap was the perfect activity for a lazy Sunday, Mom, and Beegee, could not agree more. I was digging around the top shelf of a cabinet when I felt Rhett standing in the doorway.

"Need help?" he asked as I struggled to reach the two bud vases located in the very back.

I turned and raised my eyebrow, "What was your first clue?"

Rhett grinned, chuckling, and grabbed the two glass containers for me.

"Boy, Aunt Jean can really stop a conversation, can't she?" he remarked as he sat them on the counter. I knew that she had the attention of the entire table with her comments, but I was surprisingly relieved when my husband spoke up at that moment.

"Oh, my God! Can you believe her? I don't think I've ever been struck nearly speechless like that before," I declared.

Rhett shook his head, "No disrespect intended, but is she losing her mind?"

"I'm beginning to think so…that was so…" I searched for the words.

"White-washed racism between family…to quote our son," he replied.

"Yeah…something like that," I nodded and placed the roses in the thin vases. "She hasn't always been like that, right? I mean…am I missing something?"

As I turned back to face him, Rhett wrapped his arms around my waist, pulling me close.

"No…" he shook his head, "She's just becoming a crazy old bat…"

"Well, lord help me if I got those genes," I mused as I stared into his blue eyes.

He smiled wryly, "Nah…I don't think you'll ever get old, kid."

"Oh, gee thanks for that sir," I faked offense as he laughed loudly and kissed me on the lips.

"God, get a room…" a familiar voice laughed behind us. I looked around my husband's shoulder to see Remy standing in the doorway.

"If memory serves, the last time you made that suggestion to us, we had Stacia nine months later," Rhett laughed.

"Oh God…no…you can stop," Remy chortled then paused, "Hey…I think I'm going to hit the road early…there are storms headed this way and I'd rather be strapped down by the time they reach the campground."

"Oh…okay…" I said, "But Mom just laid down…she'll be upset if you leave and don't say goodbye."

"Jera, who am I, Jack? I already talked to her…I should be back in about six weeks," he said as he hugged me. "Sooner if you need me…seriously, you call me. I'm back here in hours…I mean it."

"I know," I said and hugged my brother again. He

shook Rhett's hand and left. I instantly felt drained of energy and my husband knew it. He wrapped me up in his arms again.

"Are you going to be like this when the kids leave too?"

I could hear the ornery grin on his face.

"Yes, and suspect you'll give me shit about it," I giggled as he kissed me again.

12

May 30

The short hacking coughs of my mother could be heard throughout the house. It had been a little over two weeks since the incident on Mother's Day when we first heard what could only be described as a wet and painful sound. Mom assured me it wasn't as bad as it may have sounded but that didn't stop me from making a follow-up appointment with Dr. Mbaye. I took her in immediately for blood work and a CT scan and waited as patiently as possible for this day to come to hear the results. But I would have plenty of distractions to keep me occupied, as school was finally out for the summer which meant I would have Rhett and Stacia around a little more during the daytime. Under normal circumstances, I would have included Harrison in my summer support team, but he was working full-time at his job for the summer in preparation for college.

COLLEGE.

Ten days ago, my baby boy graduated from high school. Proud does not even come close to being an accurate word for how I felt that afternoon as I watched the *man* Rhett and I raised walk across a stage and be handed his diploma. Being a former educator, I have attended many of these ceremonies in the past so I knew what to expect. But it's so much different when it's your child in that cap and gown. Afterward, and at Harrison's request, we fired up the grill and had a cookout with all of the family in attendance.

Well, everyone *except* Jack.

Mom nor I had heard from him since brunch at Savannah's. To be completely honest, I always felt a lot less stressed when my brother and I weren't speaking. I knew he was pissed off that I "allowed" our mother to drink the champagne that day as he had made that very clear in the parking lot before he and Elaine took off. And while I felt utter relief at his absence, Mom felt unnecessarily guilty as if his behavior was her fault.

And I hate that more than anything.

But I couldn't allow his absence to get in the way of Mom's routine or her health. After Rhett helped me load her in the Tahoe, I decided I would have the difficult conversation about Jack with her; captive audience and all that.

"Mom…you seem down, what's the matter? Are you still upset about Jack?" I asked.

Her eyes never moved from her gaze out the window, "Well…I guess I must have upset him…otherwise, he would've called me by now." Her voice softened more, "I just can't figure out what I did though." Her tone was dripping with sadness and remorse.

Now, I'm really mad.

"Mom, listen to me…you haven't done anything. Are you hearing me?" I tried to catch her eye as I kept mine on the road.

"Mom, I'm serious. Jack is an asshole…"

"Jera Elizabeth! I can't believe you…" she tried to interrupt me, but I pushed back.

"No, mom…open your eyes…Jack has always thought he was better than everyone. I don't know why…and honestly, I don't care why anymore. What I care about is him making you feel bad for absolutely no reason! It's ridiculous," I charged.

"Jera…your brother loves you…"

"No, mom…my brother loves himself…he tolerates me…and he doesn't even give Remy that. I'm so tired of him being…a fucking bully!" I raised my voice to just under a shout.

My mother got quiet as she stared at me. It took her a moment before she calmly said, "I don't like that word."

I took a deep breath.

"I know… Mom…but everything I've said is the truth…you know it," I replied softly.

She nodded as tears slid down her rosy cheeks, "I do know it, Jera. I don't know why Jack is the way he is…but he's my *son*…I just want my kids to get along. Is that too much to ask?"

Goddamn it…I made my mom cry. Now, who's the asshole? Fuck you, Jack.

"Mama, I would agree with you, you know I would…but Jack doesn't want to get along…he just wants to be the boss. Rem and I get along great…but we both have issues with Jack…he's the common denominator…I just…" I paused as I pulled the truck into a parking spot in front of the hospital, "I just want you to stop beating yourself up for his actions…he's an adult…he's made his own decisions…you have done *nothing* wrong."

I reached over and took my mother's hand. Her long fingers were bony, and arthritis had set in the knuckles a long time ago. They were the hands of someone who had worked hard for a lifetime but were still surprisingly soft to the touch. I traced a protruding vein that ran along the top and down her index finger with my own then kissed the back of her hand.

"I love you Mom," I whispered.

"I love you too, sis," she whispered back.

The white walls of the waiting room that day seemed stark and colder, and it was unusually empty except for Mom and me. We sat quietly as a daytime talk show played softly on the television located in the far corner of the room. I flipped through two gardening magazines before I realized we were well past our appointment time. I looked over to my mother and found her dozing, her eyelids falling heavily before she fought to open them again. I checked the clock on the wall and realized we had been waiting for well over an hour.

"Excuse me?" I cleared my throat as I approached the front desk.

"Yes?" the young blonde receptionist looked up.

I smiled, "My mother and I have been waiting over an hour…can you find out when we will be called back?"

Apparently, this was a startling revelation to her as her eyes widened and she began to busy herself at the computer, "I am so sorry…let me check."

She clicked on her keyboard for another moment, stared at the screen, then frowned. I watched as her eyes seemed to read lines of text and she clacked on the console again.

"Ms. McKay…it seems you have arrived a day early…your mother's appointment is tomorrow," her voice was apologetic.

I shook my head, "No, I made this appointment with Darcy…she said today."

I began flipping through my phone for my email…I know I'm tired and I admittedly probably haven't eaten enough, but I don't forget my mother's medical appointments.

"I'm sorry ma'am…But the notes on the computer show your appointment is tomorrow…May 31," she countered.

I raised my phone where the receptionist could see the screen, "Here is my confirmation…May 30, 10:00 a.m."

Evidently, this was not what she wanted to see or hear, and her voice became testy, "Ma'am…I'm sorry you came all this way, but your mother's appointment is tomorrow. You will have to come back…"

"Oh, no…you see, this is clearly a mistake on someone here…not mine, not my mother's," I interrupted, trying to remain polite, "I have a confirmation for today and we were checked in…I need you to find out when we will be seeing Dr. Mbaye, today."

"Ma'am…" the receptionist began.

I smiled again, "Whitney, is it? Whitney, as you can see there has been a clerical mistake somewhere along the line. I am asking you to please get a supervisor to straighten this out…I'll wait."

I stared at the young woman until she rolled her chair back and left her station. I waited for several minutes for her to return and almost returned to my seat when an older woman, about my mother's height with dark auburn hair, sauntered to the window.

"Ms. McKay?" she drawled.

"Yes."

"Ms. McKay, it will just be a few more moments and we'll call you back for Dr. Mbaye…it seems as though there was some sort of mix-up with your appointment and the doctor went on his rounds in the main part of the hospital. I've recalled him and he'll be here in just a few minutes…if you want to have a seat, we'll take you back in a moment," her southern accent was like warm tea and honey.

"Thank you so much," I nodded cordially and returned to where my mother sat. She looked pensive and had begun wringing her hands.

"Mom? What's the matter?" I asked and sat in the seat next to her wheelchair.

"Oh…oh…" she stammered.

I looked at her puzzled, "Mom? What's going on?"

"I woke up and you weren't here…just worried me is all," she whispered.

"It's okay…I was just finding out what was taking so long," I reached out and took her hand. "It's just going to be a few more minutes."

Twenty minutes passed and I returned to the

window.

I found Whitney back at her station clicking away on her keyboard.

"Excuse me?" I said sweetly.

Her eyes looked up at me.

"Hello…we are still waiting for Dr. Mbaye. Is there any way I can get a closer ETA?" I asked. This time, she picked up the phone, dialed two numbers, and waited.

"Ms. McKay is still waiting up…oh. Okay one moment," she said into the handset before raising her eyes back to me, "The doctor is in his office…they should have already called you back. Just through the door to the left."

I sighed heavily as I turned to retrieve my mother. We made our way down the short hall and as we took the first left turn, a nurse was waiting for us.

"Right in here," she held her hand out to indicate a room to our right. As we entered, Dr. Mbaye was already seated at the small desk. He stood to greet us.

"Miss Evelyn, Miss Jera…I am so sorry about the mix-up. Please accept my apologies," he said sincerely and took Mom's hand to shake it. My mother's demeanor instantly brightened.

"Well…we won't worry about that," she batted her eyes at him.

Jesus, what a flirt.

Still holding her hand, he smiled sweetly at her, "You are too kind…Now, shall we talk?"

Dr. Mbaye allowed me to get seated before he continued, "Ms. Evelyn, as you know, we treated you with a form of direct radiation back in February for the tumor on your lung. That treatment only went so far to treat the type of cancer you have…" The cadence of his voice was rhythmic.

"However, it appears that the tumor is beginning to grow again ever so slightly," he explained.

"Meaning?" I pressed.

Concern graced his chocolate eyes, "Meaning…if Miss Evelyn refuses a more aggressive type of treatment, I'm afraid there isn't anything else we can do."

A rock the size of Montana appeared in my throat.

"I know this is not the answer you are looking for…but I promised you from the beginning, Miss Evelyn, I would be straight with you," he reached for her hand once more. "A decision does not need to be made today in this office…but I would caution you that one will need to be made by the end of the week."

I paused for a long moment trying to gather my thoughts which was difficult as time seemed to stop right then. My mother was going to die. Lung cancer would wreak its havoc on her body and rip away the life and soul of this woman. It would grow like a parasite, attaching itself to her tender organs until her small frame could not contain it any longer.

How do I respond to this?

Do I cry?

Do I scream?

Do I beg her to fight this enemy with every last breath of her existence? She asked my father to, and he obliged her until his withering bones took their final breath. Mom and I had this talk late last year when the testing began. She stated then, at her age, it was quality over quantity of life; she didn't want to live out her final days, months, or years ill from the effects of the treatments meant to extend her life.

My mind raced when I realized Dr. Mbaye was

speaking to me.

"Miss Jera? Are you alright? I know this is all shocking…"

"No, no…I'm…fine," I lied, swallowing hard. I turned to my mom but instead of being upset or even unnerved at the prospect of her impending death, she was smiling.

"Mom?" I prodded her.

She blinked at me, "Yes dear?"

I looked from Dr. Mbaye back to her, "Did you hear what he said? If you don't go into treatment, the cancer is going to keep spreading…you…you know what that means…"

She smiled sweetly at me and patted my hand with her free one–no way she was letting go of his–and said, "I heard him very clearly, Jera. But I said before…I won't do that chemotherapy. If the Lord wants me to go, I'll go."

I stared at her for another moment, reading the determination in her eyes. She had made up her mind, there would be no more treatments. I nodded to her that I understood and turned back to the doctor.

"I think she's made her decision…she won't be doing any other treatments," I fought the lump in my throat.

Dr. Mbaye nodded, "Alright then. For now, you will keep living your life as you see fit, Miss Evelyn." He turned to me, "There is assistance for you at this point…palliative care can be a welcome relief to caregivers. They will provide all of her medications along with supplies she may need…and a nurse will come by to check on her once or twice a week. I'll have Darcy set you up for a meeting. I strongly suggest you look into this type of help…this seems to be…

aggressive."

"I appreciate it," I replied.

"Miss Evelyn…if you need anything, you have your wonderful daughter call me, okay?" he spoke again to Mom.

"I will, thank you for everything," she resumed her shameless flirtation.

My mind was on another planet as I rolled Mom out of the office and through the stark walls. I helped her back into my truck and our drive home was silent with the exception of road noise. We barely spoke when I helped her into the house and retrieved her walker and I was having a difficult time concentrating on anything but the throbbing drum that was beating in my head. Once I knew she was settled for a nap, I climbed the stairs to my own bedroom.

I had a dozen phone calls I needed to make. I needed to plan dinner and run a load of laundry. The garden Rhett and I planted this spring had to be weeded and watered. But at this moment, I was absolutely too mentally exhausted to move and the thought of trying to tick any of those tasks off my list rendered me motionless. I didn't want to think about today, I didn't want to think about tomorrow. I just wanted the rock in my throat to leave and the thumping in my brain to cease. I laid my head on my pillow and closed my eyes as the silent tears fell like rivers.

***

The floating sensation I felt was euphoric. I couldn't remember the last time I felt that relaxed. I felt nothing but the softness of the fleece blanket that had just been laid on me.

I sat straight up in bed.

"Hey…I didn't mean to wake you," Rhett's voice was soothing in its tenor.

I shook the cobwebs out of my head, "No…no, it's okay. What time is it anyway?"

"A little after five…"

"Five!?" I shouted. "Oh my God…I need to start dinner." I threw the blanket off and swung my legs over the edge of the bed.

"Whoa…wait a second…" Rhett held his hands up to stop me and started looking me over with concern, "Dinner's taken care of…I grilled steaks and Stacia's finishing a salad. What's going on?"

"What do you mean? I overslept…" I realized instantly that I sounded defensive.

He knelt down in front of me and whispered, "I mean, it's not like you to nap…and this…" Rhett's hand was warm on my face as he rubbed his thumb next to my eye. "Your makeup is running…"

It felt like my heart exploded as I burst into tears, "She's gonna die, Rhett…the…tests…the tumor is growing…I…she doesn't want…" I continued to sob into my husband's chest as he wrapped me in an embrace.

"Shhh…it's okay…baby, I'm so sorry," he soothed. Rhett continued to hold me for what seemed like hours as I cried. It felt good to get it out and when I was ready, he released me, wiping my face with a tissue.

"She doesn't want the treatments, right?" he confirmed.

I shook my head.

He paused, pursing his lips, "After watching what your dad went through…I see her thinking…she just wants to enjoy the time she has left."

"I get it," I sniffled, "And it's completely *her* decision…just doesn't make it any easier."

"I know," he nodded. "What did Rem say?"

I shook my head, "I haven't talked to him yet…or anyone else. I wasn't in the right mindset when we came home…"

"Hey…Stacia and I will finish dinner and get your mom set up…call your brother…then see how it goes." Rhett kissed the side of my head as he rose, "Love you."

I gave him a short smile, "I love you too."

One ring.

Two rings.

I anticipated a third, but Remy was quick today, "Hey Jer…what's the word?"

My brother was anxious.

"Hey," I replied weakly.

I heard him holding his breath, "You've been crying…that bad? The cancer?"

"Yeah…tumor is growing again. Mom… doesn't want any other treatments…quality over quantity, you know?" I said softly and drew in a breath.

Remy coughed as he tried to speak but I knew my brother was fighting back tears of his own and it broke my heart.

"How long?" he asked.

"No idea, Rem…Dr. Mbaye thinks it could be a year…maybe less," I answered.

"Fuck!" My brother yelled out, dissolving into sobs.

There weren't very many moments in our life when I had seen my twin cry. Even as a small child, Remy was always stoic and stone-faced; he was a master at bottled feelings that usually resulted in nervous laughter and jokes. The last time I had heard him this upset came when he and Katie had lost their child. I knew this outburst was something that he had been hiding for a long time. The line became quiet, and I wondered if we were still connected.

"Rem…you still there?" I asked.

I heard him clear his nose, "Yeah…yeah, I'm here. So…what now?"

I sighed, "I've got a meeting with Johnson Regional Hospice next week…we're going to get set up with a weekly nurse and some other supports that will help her out. After that…we're just going to live life…that's all we can do."

"Do I need to come home?" he asked pointedly.

"No Rem," I chuckled, "Mom is good right now…most everything will stay the same…I'm going to make her comfortable and happy with the time she has left. You need to work and keep your schedule…if things get worse while you're out, I promise…I'll call."

"You talked to Jack?" his voice tight.

I shook my head, "No…I might save him for last..."

"No…" he cut me off, "I'll call him…we both need to be adults in this."

"Rem…you don't…"

"Stop, Jera…just…let me do this…for you," Remy said softly.

"I appreciate it," I replied, said my goodbyes, and hung up the phone.

One down and what felt like dozens more to go; but I'd save my sounding board for last.

"Oh, Jer, I'm so sorry…" I could hear the tears in Holly's voice.

"Thanks," I softly replied.

"How did Rem take the news?" she asked.

I sighed, "Not well…he cried, Hol."

"Jesus. That bad, huh?"

"Yeah."

Holly then took a deep breath, "Well…what now? Hospice?"

"Yeah, I meet with them next week…not going out as much will make it easier on Mom. The cough gets really bad when she moves too much sometimes…and with the summer humidity coming, she'll be more comfortable anyway," I explained.

"Good," she paused as I heard a break in our call, "Damn it…I got to go. Charlie's calling again."

"Wait. Why?" I pressed. I felt like I was missing something. Holly's ex-husband, Charlie had been a deadbeat pain in the ass since their divorce five years ago, but in the past year, he had been relatively quiet. I felt like a terrible friend for not asking already about the kids but, I could hear the eye roll as my friend spoke.

"He wants money. Did you know that when you don't pay your child support on time or *at all* in this state, they want to send you to jail?! Oh, the horror," her voice oozed sarcasm.

"I thought he had a good job now?" I asked.

"Oh, yeah, well…you can only get paid for working *when you show up*," the mockery of her idiot ex sent me into fits of giggles.

"So, he's behind in support, the state wants him to go to jail and he wants you to go to court and forgive the back payments…again?" I stated factually.

"Bingo," she replied, "And…he's seeing a counselor slash life coach."

"You've got to be kidding me," I snorted.

"Oh, I wish I were…"

"For what?" I demanded.

"To help him get his life in order...or at least that's what he said when I laughed and asked that same question," Holly chuckled.

"So, he can't pay for his kids, but he can afford a life coach?" I asked incredulously. "Rhett would be more than happy to be his life coach...for free."

Holly burst into raucous guffaws, "Hell, I'd be willing to pay for that myself."

The phone sounded out again and I realized she needed to deal with him. We said our goodbyes with Holly promising she would bring the kids by this weekend to see Mom. I placed the phone on the receiver and sighed again. My brain felt like putty and my head was pounding again. The smell of grilled steak wafted through the house and my stomach began to rumble as I realized I hadn't eaten all day. I started out of my bedroom when the phone rang. Like a dummy, I didn't check the caller ID before I picked up the receiver.

"Hello?"

"Hey, Jera...what the hell is going on? Why did I have to hear from Jeremy that Mom is sick?" Jack yelled.

"First of all, Jack, don't yell at me. My day has been hard enough without shit from you...second," I paused, "Rem volunteered to call you as a way of helping me with all of this fucking responsibility...believe me, it took a lot for him to do it."

"Why is that? Why would it take *a lot* for him to pick up a phone?" Jack bit back. "Is he drunk or high?"

I laughed wildly, "You're kidding, right? Well, for starters, you've treated him like complete trash our entire lives..."

"That's bullshit Jera and you know it," he cut me off.

I heard Rhett's solid footsteps ascend the carpeted stairs outside our bedroom and seconds later, he appeared in our doorway with the cordless extension in his hand.

Apparently, he picked it up before I did.

"And don't be such a brat, Jera. You sound so put upon when you bitch about the responsibility of caring for Mom…you made a choice. You chose to invite her into your home…don't complain about it now. Mom could have just as easily gone into a home where she could be looked after…"

It was my turn.

"…And cared for," I snapped. "Yeah, and when I was forced to put her in that *caring* home, they almost killed her, Jack. And yes, I made a goddamn choice…I chose my family over my career…something you've *never* done, Jack!"

"I have taken care of my family!" he charged.

I looked up and saw Rhett's eyes burn with rage, but I shook my head at him. He tossed the extension on the bed next to me and gave me *the* look; the one that spoke volumes and said I could take care of this, or he would.

"You've thrown money at your family…that's not exactly taking care of them. You barely changed a diaper," I spat.

"Don't you dare talk about what you don't know about, Jera," Jack howled angrily.

"Oh Jack…that's rich, coming from you…at least I was a parent to my kids…and now I'm a parent to *our*

Mom. Maybe you're the one that needs to shut up about things you don't have any idea about," I countered.

"You're a bitch, Jera! How dare you talk about my kids…I was always a Dad…"

"No, Jack…you got your kids every other weekend and a week in the summer…and that's *if* you weren't on a business trip or vacation with whatever new whore you were banging at the time. That's not being a twenty-four-seven-three-sixty-five parent…so, you'll excuse me if I don't take *your* advice or lack of knowledge to the bank!" I challenged angrily.

The air was silent for a moment.

"Fuck you, Jera," Jack's voice was heavy with contempt.

I didn't care.

"Back at you, big brother." And I slammed the phone down on the receiver. I drew in a deep breath and realized that my husband was still standing right outside the door. I left my place on the edge of the bed and met him in the hallway. A small grin pulled at the corner of his mouth.

"Feel better?" he asked.

"Much," I replied as we made our way to join our family already enjoying dinner.

13

June 9

Remy was still fuming about our brother's last phone call to me. I assured him every night when he checked in not to worry about Jack and made sure to reiterate that he didn't call him for any reason. It sounds completely stupid, but I didn't want Remy to have to deal with Jack's idiocy or say something he might regret.

Yeah, I know…I'm not his big sister, but I still feel protective over him. I won't apologize for that. We defended each other against Jack for most of our lives.

Jack, on the other hand, had taken a little over a week to stew about our last conversation before he decided to come to see Mom. Unfortunately for me, he came on the first day of hospice service. My house was bustling with activity when I saw his car pull into my driveway. When it did, I immediately became nauseated, and my heart raced. I didn't have the patience for another round with him.

He knocked firmly much like a door-to-door salesman and Beegee barked eagerly. I opened it and invited him in.

"What's with all the cars?" he asked. I could tell his voice was strained. He didn't want to speak to me, but he had no choice, it was my home.

"Hospice is bringing in supplies…Mom's new nurse is here," I motioned for him to follow me into the living room and watched as his entire body tensed.

"What's the matter now, Jack?" I whispered.

His cold eyes cut from side to side, "Why is she in hospice? You need to make her have the treatments."

"We've been through this…it's her body…her life…she doesn't want to do the treatments, and no one is going to force her," I growled.

"This is stupid, Jera," he whispered harshly.

"Jack, I'm warning you…don't give her shit about this…"

"You're *warning* me?" he cut me off.

At that moment, a stocky man in green medical scrubs walked up behind me and cleared his throat.

"Ma'am?" he said aloud.

I turned on my heel, "Yep! Whatcha need?"

"Just need your signature on this list," he handed me a clipboard, "I'll be back out next week and bring refills. If you need something before, just call the office and one of us will make a stop."

I signed his inventory sheet, smiled, and turned up the charm, "Thanks so much Michael…we'll see you next week!"

I turned my back on the conversation with my brother, walking into the living room to check on Mom. The nurse was just finishing her assessment and packing her stethoscope in a backpack when we entered the room.

"There are my kids! Hello son!" Mom said brightly and held her hands up to encourage Beegee to hop into her lap.

"Which one is this, Evelyn?" the nurse, a tall, blonde woman named Tammy asked.

"This is my oldest, Jack...son, this is the new woman in charge of me, Tammy," Mom introduced the pair.

Jack held out his hand politely, "Nice to meet you."

The pair shook hands and Tammy finished packing her bag, "Okay Evelyn, I'll see you next week...I'm going to talk to Jera for a minute. See you later!"

She motioned for me to follow her to the foyer; Jack trailing behind us both. When we arrived, Tammy turned to the pair of us.

"I had a really good talk with her...she was able to answer all my questions really well...my only immediate concern is that when I asked her about who was in charge of her affairs, she said she hadn't thought about it. Now, of course, it's not an immediate concern...but I thought I would put it out to you so you all can open up the conversation before the inevitable happens," she explained.

"Oh...okay...yeah, I'll talk to her about it," I said, opening the door.

"Good!" She replied, "Have a great day...see you next week."

Jack and I walked silently back into the living room. He sat next to mom, and they talked for around an hour before she became tired and wanted to lie down. Stacia, who had been waiting for her grandma to just say the word, helped mom to the restroom and into her bed. After Jack knew she was comfortable, he rose to leave.

"I'll get out of here…I'll be back next week to have that talk with Mom about her *affairs*, as that nurse puts it," he remarked.

I frowned then shrugged my shoulders, "Alright…"

"Will you be here?" he asked shortly.

"Well, my house…good chance in that," I replied.

"Hmm," he nodded and strode out the door.

14

June 14

A few days went by, and Mom never mentioned anything about what she and the nurse had spoken about. I honestly wanted to broach the subject before my brother could charge in and demand she makes decisions. Mom was still very much in her right mind and very strong-willed. She has never been one to be pushed around, but I feared that my brother's particular brand of brashness would go over like a lead balloon, as they say.

I was right.

Jack didn't make it a week before he showed up on my doorstep with the power of attorney paperwork in hand. He promptly sat down in front of our mother and strongly urged her to sign the documents.

"Why?" she asked as she stroked Beegee's slender head.

"Because Mom…you don't have anything in writing. This will help everyone in the long run…especially since you have made the asinine decision to not fight this disease," he replied.

Ooo. Not the best choice of words, Jack; but please continue.

"Asinine?" she seemed to be clarifying his meaning.

"Mom…maybe that's not the right word…but you *do* understand that you're just checking out, right? Seems kind of cowardly," he continued.

Oh…this was going to be good. This idiot brother of mine not only implied Mom's decision about her own body was invalid, but he now called her a coward. It's like he's never met this woman or doesn't remember his own childhood.

When Jack was about thirteen, there was a neighborhood bully that seemed hyper-focused on tormenting my brother. One afternoon, the kids were standing in our front yard when this little jerk threw a handful of rocks at Jack's face. One of the rocks was quite large and gave him a decent-sized goose egg that instantaneously grew from his forehead. Jack didn't cry or yell out; he just punched this kid squarely in the mouth. Before we knew it, the bully ran home crying to his mother, who came down to have words with our mother.

Unfortunately for her, Mom had watched the entire ordeal play out from our front window. So, when the mother came screaming into our yard and slapped Jack across the face for "Beating up her precious boy,", it was game over. Our mother, Mrs. Evelyn Northland, and all of her five-foot, one-inch frame climbed the back of the bully's mother like a tree and beat the shit out of her.

Did I forget to mention that she's kind of a badass?

"It's like you're not even trying, Mom. You need to fight this," he smiled at her in a way that begged for her to agree with him. She glanced down at the paperwork he placed on her lap.

"What is this?" she asked him calmly and shooed the dog from her lap.

"This is a durable power of attorney...it's the paperwork you need to sign to put someone in charge of your affairs," he explained.

Mom put her reading glasses on and began to skim the forms. I sat across from the pair of them on the sofa quietly, sipped my Diet Coke, and waited for her to respond. I could be completely wrong about this entire situation, and she might change her mind about treatment. My mom wasn't unreasonable, and she had always been a down-to-earth, levelheaded human being. It's possible that she would take unsolicited advice from her son.

And the next winter Olympics could take place in hell.

After a moment of reading, Mom removed her glasses and placed them on her lap with the documents, then folded her hands on top. Her normally sparkling blue eyes seemed to turn to steel as she narrowed them on my brother.

"I see you have taken the liberty of filling the paperwork out for me," she commented coolly.

"Well, I thought it would expedite everything," he replied.

"I see," her voice short. "Well, despite your efforts, son, your assistance with this matter is not needed."

"What?" Jack blinked then shot a dangerous glance in my direction.

Hey…whatever he was thinking, I had nothing to do with it; this was news to me too.

"You heard me…and don't look at your sister like that. She has no idea what I'm about to say," Mom's voice was firm, and I had not heard her speak in that tone since we were kids. "Jackson Robert Northland, I'm going to tell you something, so you listen up…"

Damn. She middle-named him.

"I'll have you know that all of my "affairs"," she made air quotes with her fingers, "Are already in order and have been for many years. *You* think I'm some sort of imbecile…my decisions about my own care are…asinine, to use your word, and that I'm a coward? Well, son, once you've lived as long as I have and have walked the paths that I have you can lecture me on what I should and shouldn't do!" Her voice filled the room as it thundered, and she paused for a moment to allow her words to sink in and to catch her breath.

"After your father died and after I was diagnosed with MS, I set up a living trust on my estate…I also named your sister as my power of attorney," her words came out measured and calmer.

Jack's head flipped to my spot on the sofa, and he glared at me; however, a normal person would have seen that I was just as shocked as my brother. After a second, he turned back to our mother.

"Why?! Why did you pick Jera? Don't you think I would have been a better choice?" he asked in angry astonishment.

"I picked who I thought would do the best job," Mom shrugged.

The comment seemed to set my brother on fire, and he threw himself out of the chair to stand in front of our Mom. He then did something that, if I had not seen for myself, I would've never believed: he stomped his foot like a petulant child.

"*I* would be the better choice, Mom," he yelled, "You should trust my judgment over hers or that brother of mine…I am your number one son!"

Our mother stared at Jack. There wasn't a touch of disbelief on her face as to what she was witnessing, unlike me, and it was almost as if she expected this reaction. My mouth gaped and I couldn't move as I watched the live soap opera play out in my own living room.

"Jack…I believe I made the right choice. Out of the three of my children, she is the most fair…she will make sure my wishes are followed…no matter what…I know that. I can't expect Jeremy to remain neutral regarding you after you have called him names your whole life…Jera is the right choice," she stated as a matter of fact.

Jack was furious, "Fine…if that is how you feel about me…"

"No, son…this isn't a popularity contest. I love you with my whole heart…but son…it's not about you…this is about me," she replied. The room was quiet as their conversation marinated.

Jack only nodded then bent down to kiss our mother on the cheek. Her arthritic hands held his face as she whispered, "I love you, Jack."

Another surprise came when I heard him whisper back, "I love you, Mom."

Jack left and didn't return to visit for three weeks.

But none of that mattered because our Mom had spoken. She was going to live out the rest of her life by her own rules. She didn't need anyone, especially her children, to make those major decisions for her. I have always respected my mom, but that day I knew in my heart that no matter how much time we had left with her it would never be enough. That day I promised myself and her to make every day exactly what she wanted it to be…and to hell with anyone who would obfuscate her peace.

15

June 24

Mine and Rhett's twenty-fifth wedding anniversary.

I almost couldn't believe it had been twenty-five years since we married; but of course, we had been together more like thirty. Since leaving the Marines, it had been Rhett's habit to have an early morning run before getting ready for the day. I could hear the shower still running in our master bathroom meaning he must have thrown in an extra mile today. As I waited for him to exit, I sat on the edge of our bed thinking of all the things we had accomplished, all the laughter, and even all the tears that had been shed over these years. The list was long and memorable.

In these twenty-five years, we had both graduated college and embarked on our careers. Actually, in that time, my husband had two careers. We have lived together in three states and Rhett had actually lived in countless types of housing in places near and far. I gave birth to two babies in two years. We nurtured and fed and guided those children through all of life's phases to this point and now they had become young adults, who would eventually do the same for their children. I thought about the first vacation we took as a family to an amusement park located in a tourist town two hours from our home. We ate corn dogs and funnel cakes and rode on rides designed to test the nerves—and a person's intestinal integrity. I remembered the color of green the then seven-year-old Stacia's face became when she hopped down off the park's version of the teacup ride after her second bag of popcorn. And how much the eight-year-old Harrison loved the enormous Viking boat swing that made him feel like he was flying.

We watched three of our four of our grandparents leave this world and an aunt and uncle, or two. We witnessed my own father succumb to the unrelenting and overpowering tyrant that is cancer. We mourned with my brother when he and his wife lost their child. We were overjoyed when we saw friends marry and were devastated when those relationships crumbled into divorce. Through all of those bits of hardship and despair, our home became a beacon for laughter, safety, and a friendly shoulder to lean on. I smiled to myself thinking about where we started and now, where we were going. I was completely lost in my own daydreams and didn't hear the water shut off, jumping when Rhett's damp hand touched my shoulder.

"Hey…didn't mean to scare you…lost in a thought?" he smiled as he dried his short-cropped hair with a towel.

"Yeah…just thinking about our life, where we've been," I mused.

Rhett took up a place next to me, "We've definitely

seen some things." He leaned into my shoulder, "You know, we've got a lot more to see."

"I know," I turned to him, smiling, "Twenty-five years…I can't believe I've put up with you that long."

He grinned in mock offense, "*You* put up with *me?*" He paused then shrugged, "Yeah, you're probably right…"

I saw the mischief cross his eyes before he walked back toward the bathroom.

"But when we get in front of that divorce judge…"

"Divorce judge!?" I cried out laughing.

"Hell yeah…irreconcilable differences," he chuckled.

"Oh yeah? What's that?" I teased as I rose and slowly made my way toward him.

"'Your honor…I couldn't possibly stay married to this woman for two reasons…the blocks of ice she calls feet that she likes to put in my back and…" he paused again, "She snores."

"You wouldn't!?" I giggled and leaped after him, pulling the towel from around his waist and leaving him completely naked.

"Hey!" he laughed.

It's here where I feel like I need to tell you that my husband is what you would call…*hot*. I'm not just saying that because I love him with my entire soul but because it is absolutely true. And the older he gets, the more I'm attracted to him. Is it his bright blue eyes? Maybe. Is it the grey hair that is sprinkled like confetti on his head and around his temples? Possibly. Tight ass? That's a start but I'll be honest, the most attractive, *physical* part about Rhett is he, still at forty-seven, has dad abs of steel. There's a little age weight there, but seriously…this man is still cut.

We laughed as we played keep away with his towel. Eventually, I was thrown into a fit of giggles, and he took his opportunity to throw me over his shoulder, then onto the bed.

"Okay! Okay! I give up!" I threw the cover at him.

He tossed it on the floor and lay next to me, pulling me into his chest. His body was still warm from the shower, and I ran my hands over his soft skin. I drew a deep breath and took in every scent of him. As I looked up, we fell into long kisses that made my toes curl. After several minutes, I finally pulled away and shook my head.

"Sir…we don't have time for…*activities*…right now," I smiled.

"No? Well…I guess we'll just have to pause this until later," he grinned suspiciously.

I eyed him, "What is… later?"

He pursed his lips, gave me a quick peck on the cheek, then retrieved his towel from the floor. He shrugged.

"Rhett Michael McKay…what did you do?" I laughed.

"You'll see."

That was the only answer I was going to get. My husband dressed quickly and left me alone on the bed.

Mom was still sleeping with Beegee at the foot of the bed when I checked on her after my shower. She had always been an early riser from as far back as I can remember, but in the past couple of months, she had been gradually adding a few minutes every morning of a little extra shut-eye. I busied myself with breakfast and a cup of coffee while I waited for her to wake. I sat at my dining table working on a shopping list when I heard a familiar rumble making its way up my drive.

As I walked to the front windows of the living room, I saw Remy's truck stop in its usual spot.

"What the hell?" I said under my breath.

Rhett, who sat on the sofa sipping coffee laughed, "Oh…Did I forget to mention your brother will be in this weekend?"

I shot a narrowed-eyed look at my husband.

"I must have," he shrugged. About that time, I saw Remy step up on the porch and I flung open the door.

"What are you doing here?" I asked as I threw my arms around his shoulders.

"Working…special assignment," he offered and threw his duffle bag on the floor next to Rhett.

"What assignment?" My suspicion grew; these guys were definitely up to something.

"Oh…need to know only. You don't have clearance," he stated flatly.

"I…don't have *clearance*…now that sounds like some Marine bs," and I again eyed my husband, who was noticeably stifling laughter.

Without looking up from his cup, Rhett spoke to my brother, "Man, if we both make it out of this day alive, we need to consider ourselves lucky…she's already losing her patience."

I rolled my eyes and walked back toward the kitchen as both men burst into laughter, "You both are insufferable…Rem…coffees' hot."

I'm not one for surprises; I mean, I love them, but I like them better when I don't know they're coming. Adding in two *adult* men giggling and whispering like pre-teen boys all day is…obnoxious. But luckily, Holly and the kids stopped by for lunch, which offered me a little distraction from whatever scheme my husband and brother had planned. In a rare event, neither

Harrison nor Stacia had to work until that evening, so I was pleasantly pleased to have a full house at around noon. At Mom's request, I made tuna salad sandwiches–peanut butter and jelly for the kids–along with pasta salad, chips, and fresh fruit. We had a great time talking and catching up with each other.

It was around four that afternoon when Rhett came into the house from working in the yard and announced that we needed to go upstairs and get ready.

I frowned, "For what?"

"Our date," he smiled.

"Rhett…we can't…Mom…" I replied quietly.

"Hey…that's why I'm here," Remy remarked from the dining table where he sat next to Holly.

She was grinning too. Were they all in on this?

"Special assignment, huh?" I snarked at my brother.

He laughed, "Yeah…I mean, twenty-five years is kinda a big deal."

I looked from Rhett to Remy, then to Holly. I was so lucky to have such a great support group, but I was also nervous. Mom had issues getting to the restroom sometimes and I would have to help her off the toilet and wipe her. Other times, she couldn't get up and would urinate in her adult brief, which would then need to be changed for a dry one. There were also her meds and then the routine of getting her ready and into bed at night. She was very particular and would rarely allow Stacia to help her with that. The only time in the past two years that we hadn't done our nightly ritual was the few weeks she spent in the nursing home this year.

I looked up at my husband, "Sweetheart, thank you for whatever you have planned…but I just don't think that this is…"

"Don't even think for a second of trying to back out," Remy ordered. "I'm perfectly capable of taking care of Mom...you *have* to let me do this. Besides...Holly is staying to help, seriously Jer...we've got this covered."

I paused again, "God you're bossy."

"Yeah, well...I am older," he laughed.

I rolled my eyes, "By ninety seconds, Rem." I allowed Rhett to take my hand and lead me to our bedroom when I heard my brother call out.

"Still makes me the older brother!"

***

At nearly five-thirty, we rolled into a parking spot in Rhett's 1970 Tiffany blue Ford Bronco. His dad had purchased the vehicle brand new and several years ago, he and Rhett had worked to restore the truck to new condition. Most of the time, it sat in our three-car garage, but this was a special occasion, and I *loved* this truck.

"Ariana's?" I confirmed, smiling.

"Good choice?" he asked as he leaned closer.

"Very good...what are we doing? Fondue or tapas?"

"Maybe a little of both," he mused before kissing me softly.

Seriously. This guy.

The evening could not have been more perfect. We sat at our corner table for three hours talking, eating, and sipping wine. Afterward, we went for a drive around the city with the windows down and the music turned up, holding hands. Around eleven, he pulled into a drive-through ice cream parlor and ordered two vanilla cones. We got out of the truck to eat and people-watch at one of several small picnic tables located out front near the walk-up windows. I was occupied watching a very young family at a nearby table trying to clean up their very excited toddler, so I didn't notice Rhett laying the deep purple, velvet box on the table between us. When I turned my eyes back to him, I saw it and looked at him, perplexed.

"What's this?" I asked.

Rhett grinned from behind his cone, "Happy Anniversary."

"You didn't…"

"Will you open it already?" he laughed, rolling his eyes. He took my cone as I wiped my hands. Reaching for the box I lifted the lid; the ring inside took my breath away. Five round diamonds sat along the length of a white gold band with a thin row of smaller stones woven between each set like a vine.

"Oh my God…Rhett! It's…" I gasped as tears fell from my eyes.

"So…you like it?" he smiled.

"It's absolutely too much…" My voice broke as I stared at the stones glistening in the harsh parking lights.

"No…it's not enough," he stated sweetly and tossed the melting dessert into the trash can next to our table. He picked up the box, freed the ring from its home, and placed it on my finger next to my engagement ring and wedding band. It was like they were made for each other.

"How…I mean…" I couldn't find my words. He tugged on my hands to bring me to his side of the table and onto his lap.

"Jera…I know this is just rocks and metal…but I wanted to get you something special. You deserve it…for everything you do. I love you more today than I did when we got married…and I know I'll love you more tomorrow," he whispered before placing his soft lips on mine.

After a few more sweet moments, we hopped back in the truck and headed to our home. When we arrived, the house was quiet, and our normal nightlights offered their soft glow as a welcome. Even though we have another small guest room, Remy was sound asleep on the sofa. I peeked into Mom's room and heard her and Beegee's soft snoring in the darkness. A note left on the kitchen table from Holly told me that everything went well and she would call me tomorrow to get all the details about my night. I smiled with a full heart as I climbed the stairs to our bedroom to continue my date with Rhett.

16

July 4

"Let me see your finger one more time," Mom said as she played with my anniversary gift from Rhett.

I laughed, "C'mon mom…we need to get you dressed. I've still got chicken to marinate and a huge watermelon to cut up before everyone gets here."

"Well, I'm just admiring your husband's good taste," she smiled as I reached behind her and connected the four hooks and eye closures on her bra.

I carefully pulled the dark blue shirt over her head before I knelt to put her feet into her shorts as Beegee licked my face, "Okay, Mom…let's stand you up and I'll pull on your pants…B! Stop it, you goofy dog."

Mom was exceptionally shaky today and it took a little more effort to get her to her feet. She swayed unsteadily, grasping her walker as I pulled up her matching shorts. I caught her by the shoulder and elbow just as she fell back on her bed.

"I think I need a minute," she puffed.

"What about a breathing treatment?" I offered.

"No…just give me a second to catch my air again," she replied. I sat next to her on the bed and rubbed her back and she closed her eyes. "That feels good sis…these old bones hurt."

After a moment, she looked over at me, "Okay, I think I'm ready now."

I eased her to her feet, and we padded slowly into the living room. I got her leaned into her mechanical recliner and lowered her slowly to a seated position, then raised her feet.

"Okay…now, I need coffee," she said.

"Yes ma'am…" I smiled down at her.

After getting her settled for the morning, I turned on her favorite daytime television before I retreated back into the kitchen to prep for our annual family Fourth of July barbeque. I anticipated our guests would be arriving in a few hours and I still had so much to prep. Luckily for me, Stacia would be home and could do any extra that needed to be taken care of. Rhett busied himself with getting the deck and patio in order, setting up the chairs, and cleaning the grill. It was around two-thirty when Holly, her six-year-old daughter, Ashton, and her four-year-old son, Jace arrived. The kids promptly gave my mother and Beegee hugs and kisses then ran in to show me the fireworks they brought with them.

"Wow! That's a lot of stuff," I said excitedly. "You should take Bee outside and give those to Uncle Rhett so he can light them for you when it gets dark."

"Okay!" they both yelled as they ran out the back door with the dog happily at their heels.

Holly sighed, "Thanks for that..."

"What's the matter?" I frowned and went back to dicing a cantaloupe.

"Charlie was supposed to come by today and *bring* them fireworks. Fucker promised them on the phone last week he would be by this morning...and guess what? He never showed," she growled, snatching a freshly cut piece of melon and popping it in her mouth.

"Shocker," I faked a gasp, my eyes wide.

Holly chuckled, "I know...I just get tired of his bullshit. How did I fall for such a goddamn loser, Jer?"

I heard Mom's feet shuffling as she crossed the threshold, "We've all done it Holly...don't worry...there's a good man waiting for you. One that works hard...handsome..."

"Thanks, Mom," Holly smiled. "Not sure I'm gonna find him here, in this town."

"Oh, well a pretty girl like you has to make the first move sometimes," she smiled. "Men come and go..."

"Hey Mom...you hungry?" I grinned. The woman had the nose of a bloodhound, and I was already putting pieces of cantaloupe on a plate.

"Well, I thought that was my lunch you were fixing," she laughed as she plopped hard into a chair.

"Oh my God...be careful!" Holly jumped, grabbing Mom by her elbow.

Holly looked at me with concern and I knew what she was thinking because I had the same thought: Mom's motor function was getting worse by the day. There was nothing I could do. Mom was a patient of hospice now and there would be no more doctor's appointments or anything else for that matter that could be seen as lifesaving. I would just have to keep an extra eye on her and pray that she didn't fall again.

We had gotten damn lucky when she had the stroke that she didn't break a hip. A fall like that would certainly cut her life shorter than it already was; I wouldn't risk that. I kept a close eye on her while she enjoyed her very light lunch of two slices of melon I chopped and lightly salted. When I noticed she was ready to return to her recliner, I called for Harrison to help.

"Hey, Mom," I got close to her so she could hear me, "Harry is going to help you to the living room."

He lifted his grandmother gently from the chair and held her close to his body for a moment.

"Grandma…you wanna dance?" he teased her.

She smiled brightly up at my six-foot-two teenager, "You're Papa and I used to dance…you're getting to be as tall as he was."

Once Harrison was convinced she was steady enough to walk, he held her around the waist until they made it to her seat, then he lowered her down.

"All aboard the geriatric coaster!" he laughed as he used the remote on her power recliner.

"You crazy kid!" Mom laughed and he glanced back at me, as I stood in the kitchen with held breath.

"You need anything else, grandma?" he asked.

"No…thank you, sweet boy," she grinned and laid her head back, closing her eyes. Harrison walked back toward me at the island.

"I'm going out to help Dad…yell if you need me," he turned, leaving out of the sliding door.

Damn it…I've got great kids.

Mom napped until the rest of our family and friends arrived. The summer sun was merciless, as was usual for Missouri this time of year, but we were all thankful for a constant breeze from the west. Rhett and his dad grilled burgers, hot dogs, and chicken while all the younger children that came played with Beegee in the two large sprinklers that had been set up at the back of our fence line earlier in the day. The purpose was twofold: it gave the smaller kids relief from the heat and also wet the ground where we would later shoot off the fireworks.

Mom chatted with Aunt Jean and Aunt Leann as I served her dinner on a TV tray at her recliner; she admitted she was too comfortable to move to the table. Luckily, after dinner, the hot afternoon turned into a pleasant night and all the kids, young and old, begged for fireworks. With Harrison and Stacia's help, Mom made her way to the deck to also enjoy the show. In the dark, we could barely see Rhett, Harrison, and Richard's silhouettes at the back of our property line as they lit the packs of explosives. Before long, the familiar smell of gunpowder and smoke filled the air. With each sparkling burst, Mom would 'ooo' and 'ahhh', several times exclaiming "That one's my favorite!"

I smiled because they were all her favorites.

It was around midnight before the last person left and I was able to finally get Mom settled on the bed once more in her nightgown. We went through our nightly routine of using the toilet, cleaning her dentures, washing her face, and brushing her hair. By the time that was all finished, she was completely exhausted.

"Okay Mom…let me get your feet in bed," I said as I bent to swipe her lower half up and onto the mattress.

"Oh…Jera…I'm so tired…" she yawned, and the

dog hopped into bed next to her.

"I know…big day…and it's after twelve. I bet you *are* tired," I replied.

Her eyes were heavy, and I could tell she would be out before I could get the covers over her.

"Maybe your dad will come get me tonight," she mumbled.

I stopped cold.

Did I hear her right?

"Mom…what did you mean by that?" I asked loudly.

"What!? What did you say?" she startled, a little more awake this time.

I paused for a long moment as she looked at me sleepily. I couldn't ask again. I couldn't ask what she meant by the comment because my heart couldn't take what I was afraid her answer would be. I covered her up and kissed her on the head.

"Good night, Mama," I whispered as hot tears flowed from my eyes.

17

July 25

It had been a crazy but quiet couple of weeks in the McKay house. A few days after our Independence Day celebrations, Rhett and five other Marine buddies took off to Colorado for their annual camping trip, this year with Harrison in tow. So, for four days, Mom, Stacia, and I had the house all to ourselves—just the girls. We had an amazing four days. Stacia and I set up a little beauty shop in the dining room and pampered Mom for an entire afternoon; hair, mani-pedi, mini massage, the entire package. Another day, we played cards for hours as my daughter and I tried like hell to beat my mother, the card shark, at Rummy. We laughed and giggled and told stories…we made connections and memories that would never, ever be forgotten.

I knew Rhett and Harrison were due back any time, so when I heard a truck pull into the driveway, I didn't think much about it. What I had forgotten is that Remy was also coming home today, so I was surprised when I heard the knock on the door.

"Hi Uncle Remy!" Stacia exclaimed.

"Hey kid…hey Bee!" He scratched the excited dog behind the ears.

"Rem! I'm so sorry…I forgot you were coming home too…Rhett and Harry will be in soon," I greeted my brother as I made my way out of the kitchen, drying my hands on a towel.

"How did the trip go?" he asked.

"Rhett said it was a great time when we spoke," I replied but was interrupted by the ringing of my cell phone. "Oh…wait a sec…it's the hospice calling…Hello?"

"Yes…This is Wyland Buckridge with Johnson Hospice. May I speak with Mrs. McKay?" a husky man's voice said.

"Yes, this is Jera McKay," I replied.

"Oh, Hello Mrs. McKay…as I said, I'm Wyland Buckridge, the director with Johnson Hospice. I'm calling regarding your mother, Evelyn Northland."

"Okay…"

"Mrs. McKay, as you know, your mother's care is reviewed weekly by the visiting nurse and administration staff…and well, it is an unfortunate situation, but we decided that your mother doesn't fit the qualifications for hospice care," he remarked.

"What?" I gasped and Remy looked at me concerned. I made my way back to the kitchen and out onto the deck outside, way out of Mom's earshot and he followed. I placed the call on speakerphone.

"Well, frankly Mrs. McKay…your mother's case is not…" Buckridge began.

"Is not what?" I cut in.

"Ma'am, its severity is not imminent…and as you know there are criteria that must be met in a palliative setting," he continued, unbothered by my interruption.

"Her severity is not imminent? Mr. Buckridge, she has *terminal cancer*," I emphasized the condition clearly, "How does that alone not meet the criteria?"

"Hey, babe…" I heard Rhett say and I turned to show him I was on the phone. glowering. He stood still and held his dirty gear as the conversation continued.

"Mrs. McKay…usually when people enter into a setting such as this, their condition is dire…that is just not the case with your mother. So…services will be terminated immediately," he said matter-of-factually.

I was completely dumbfounded. How could they do this? There was absolutely no doubt that my mom was dying. She refused treatment for her lung cancer, and we knew as the weeks went by that the tumor was growing. There would be no miracle that would save her. As if I flipped a light in a darkened room, I had an epiphany.

"So, what you're saying, Mr. Buckridge, is that my mother isn't dying fast enough for you, is that it?" I was so angry.

"No! Mrs. McKay…I would not say that…it's just her condition…"

"Let me stop you right there, Mr. Buckridge. She is dying of lung cancer. Period. You and your company were hired to care for my mother in way of palliative care until she takes her last breath…and because you've now run the numbers and know that she may have more than these past six weeks in her, you don't want to *pay* your staff for that care…fine… But I am not an idiot, Mr. Buckridge…I know how a hospice works…this isn't my only parent to have the service and you aren't my first time around the block…Shame on you and your company…and go to hell," I ended the call and could feel my face flush; and not just from the summer sun. I looked up at my brother and husband, both of which had their own looks of shock.

"What the hell just happened?" Rhett asked, eyebrows raised.

"Mother fuckers!" I exclaimed. "How dare they!"

"So, that's it? They can just cut Mom off?" Remy asked.

"I guess so…" I threw my hands up then took a deep breath. I started scrolling through my contacts and found Dr. Mbaye's office number and dialed.

"Who you calling?" Rhett asked.

"Her oncologist…I'm going to tell them what happened and ask them to find us another hospice…Mom is not losing her services," I replied calmly.

Rhett nodded and finally dropped his pack, dirt cascading off it and into the breeze. Remy turned and headed back into the house, "I'm gonna say hi to Mom."

18

July 28

It took less than twenty-four hours for Dr. Mbaye's office to request a new palliative care service and just a day and a half later, they were set up in our home. It was the quickest transition I had ever witnessed, and I was thankful for it. Mom never batted an eye when I told her that Dr. Mbaye had called Compassionate Care Hospice to come in instead of Johnson County. There was no way in hell I was telling my mother, the former nurse, the real reason we had to switch.

"He probably had a good reason…he's a smart man," she said, and her eyes twinkled when I told her. While indeed he was smart, that wasn't the real reason she liked him so much. He was tall with a brilliant smile and "Easy on the eyes".

Hey, don't judge. When you're an eighty-year-old

woman, you can objectify men too.

Her new nurse, a short woman with beautifully expressive round eyes, red lips, and curly auburn hair named Amanda, had just finished her assessment when I came inside with a basket full of tomatoes from my garden.

"Miss Evelyn looks like you just might get that BLT after all," Amanda smiled at my mother and gave me a small nod.

"Oh really? Did she get a good harvest?" Mom asked. I rounded the corner and held out a softball-sized beefsteak tomato.

"How is this?" I grinned.

Mom's eyes widened, "Oh, my…now, that looks good enough to eat. Why don't you give me a slice of that on a piece of bread and butter."

Amanda's eyes smiled, "My grannie used to eat tomato and butter sandwiches."

"Your grannie had good taste," Mom patted her hand.

"If you say so, Mom," I laughed from the kitchen. Amanda made her way to me as I prepped the sandwich.

"I just wanted to let you know that your mom is a delight and I'll be here for the long haul," she assured me.

I sat the knife down, "I guess you've been told of our situation?"

"I have," she nodded. "It's unacceptable what happened. I've read your mom's chart…and I've just listened to her lungs. They aren't good…but I don't want you to worry about any of that…we'll take good care of her."

I nodded, "Thank you…I appreciate that more than you know."

"Of course! And" she took a business card out of a holder that was attached to her cell phone, "If you need anything…don't hesitate to call me." I took the card and thanked her. She turned and headed back to the living room.

"See you in a couple of days, Miss Evelyn," her voice was bubbly, and the air was a little lighter when she left.

I was so thankful for her kind words. She was making this new road bump a little easier to handle. The part of me that was still so freshly pissed off at Johnson Hospice was getting smaller, but I knew it would never be gone. As a child, my parents weren't overly religious, but we did attend an Episcopal church just a few blocks from our home. One of the verses I remember learning about was 1 Timothy and how the love of money was the root of all evil. It rang true for me now; the evilness of corporate greed and their love of money earned on the deaths of the ill and infirm. No compassion; no charity, just greed.

I was so lost in thought that I didn't notice the silver Audi pulling next to my house. Jack was nearly on my doorstep before I realized, and I opened the door before he knocked.

"Hello," he said, the word short and staccato.

"Hey…come in…I just made Mom a sandwich," I moved to allow him to pass.

"Who just left?" he tried his best to make conversation.

"New hospice company," I began, but before I could finish, Jack cut me off.

"New hospice? Why? What's wrong with the other

one?" he demanded as Remy entered the room.

"Well, I was getting ready to say that Johnson dropped her as a client…they needed her to die faster," I remarked with dripping sarcasm.

Jack rolled his eyes, "C'mon Jera…that's not true. What *actually* happened?"

"That *is* what happened, Jack," Remy replied, and Jack's head snapped in his direction.

"I wasn't asking you," he growled, glaring at him with utter hatred.

"I don't give a damn who you're talking to," Remy chuckled angrily.

Jack took a step closer to Remy, "Listen here loser when I want your opinion, I'll ask for it…otherwise, mind your business."

He poked Remy in the chest.

Remy, never one to back down from a challenge, also took a step closer, "You know Jack, one of these days, I'm going to knock that smugness off you."

"Both of you outside!" I whispered loudly through clenched teeth. Remy turned quickly and nearly marched out of the door with Jack on his heel. As they stepped off the porch and into my yard, Jack shoved Remy's shoulder hard.

"I'm sick of your smart-ass mouth," Jack yelled. Remy spun around to square off with our brother.

"I'm just sick of you, you fucking asshole," Remy barked as he shoved Jack, hard.

"Keep your fucking hands off me," bellowed Jack as his open hand made contact with the side of Remy's face. Remy gave our brother no more warnings as he threw a punch that caught Jack in the chest. I tried to step between my brothers as they began to throw more punches.

"Goddamn, you both…stop it! Stop it now!" I screamed. From that moment, everything following happened in slow motion.

Out of the corner of my eye, I saw Rhett come around the corner of the house and run toward us, "Hey!"

As I tried to put my body between my siblings to stop their assault on each other, Jack's fist caught me in the side of the head and I tumbled back, falling hard on the ground.

"Motherfucker!" Remy bellowed, lunging for Jack once more.

"I said knock it off!" Rhett, using his best Marine voice, barked over the chaos. He grabbed Remy by the collar of his shirt and drew him back.

"You stupid fuck!" Jack screamed.

"I said enough!" Rhett's voice carried over our enormous yard and bounced off the trees. He looked between each panting man, "What the hell is going on?"

Remy swallowed hard, still trying to catch his breath, "This asshole…can't…keep his hands to himself…"

"You little prick," Jack caught his breath.

"Ok, Jack…answer me this," Rhett's eyes narrowed, "If you've got beef with Rem, why is your sister on the ground?"

Jack glowered at Rhett, "First of all, this is none of your business, *Rhett*…you're barely family…so, you need to butt out."

"Anything that involves my *wife*, *is* my business, Jack…"

"Not when it comes to my mother or her affairs…so, just take your jarhead back in the house,"

Jack interjected angrily.

Rhett laughed, which, by the look on Jack's face, was not the reaction he expected nor wanted.

"I'll ask again, *why* is my wife on the ground, Jack?" Rhett asked, his tone a little more dangerous this time.

Jack pointed a finger in my husband's face, "You know what? Fuck you Rhett…if the bitch can't mind her business, she probably deserved whatever happened."

It only took Rhett one swing and Jack was sprawled out on our lawn.

He looked down at my brother who had rolled to his side and begun to rub his face and chin, "I think you're done here today, Jack. Time for you to go home…come back and see your mother tomorrow or when you decide to start acting like an adult."

Jack stared at him for a moment before he spoke again, "Are you seriously forbidding me to see my own mother?"

Rhett's eyes widened, "Yeah, I am…you're not coming into my home with your disrespect and that chip on your shoulder. I'm done watching you make your sister's life miserable…grow up Jack…when you can act like a man, you can come back."

"You're not keeping me from seeing *my* mother," Jack growled.

"Jack, you need to cool down…just go home. Calm down, when you're ready to be civil, and apologize to your sister, you can come back," Rhett's voice was calm, but filled with unquestionable authority. Jack's eyes bounced between me on the ground and Remy's. The three of us watched as Jack quickly and quietly made his way back to his vehicle and tore down the driveway. Rhett knelt beside me and offered his hand to help me up.

"Baby, are you okay?" he asked.

"Yeah…it was my fault…I shouldn't have stepped between the two of them," I explained.

He shook his head, "No…Jack was out of line. C'mon, let's get some ice for that eye…slugger."

I laughed and a shooting pain pierced my temple.

Remy walked up to the pair of us, hanging his head, "Jer, I'm sorry…I shouldn't have pushed it with him…"

"Rem…no…this isn't your fault either. Jack's an asshole and he'll always be an asshole…he got what he deserved. He needs to cool off as much as anyone," I hugged my brother.

It took Jack a week before he called, and I received an incredibly transparent and shallow apology; then another week to show up for a visit. But at that point, I really didn't expect anything from him or want anything to do with him. I was never going to change Jack, so none of it really matters in the grand design of life. I decided that it was best to just allow the entire situation to shrink back into the recesses of memory… for now. I was more pleased that neither my children nor my Mother had witnessed what happened; I didn't want any of them involved. It was bad enough I had to lie about a bruised eye. What was important was creating a supportive environment for my mother to live out her final days, however long that would be. If that meant that Remy had to bite his tongue when Jack was around, so be it; I had done it for years. I was over the drama and wanted all of it to stop. I accepted that I would never have a real relationship with my eldest brother again, and that was probably for the best.

Life is too short to deal with shitty people.

19

September 15

Over the past month and a half, Mom's condition has deteriorated quickly. Her raspy cough was coming on more frequently and she had taken to wearing her nighttime adult diapers all of the time because it was just too hard for her to get up fast enough. She began to look paler, and her eyes had become tired. While she still enjoyed getting visitors, family members began to slowly stop coming by to chat for very long. I understood a little of it. Aunt Patty was nearly blind and hadn't driven in years. Uncle Chuck didn't handle sickness well and he hated seeing anyone being withered by a disease, but Aunt Leann still came by on occasion. Aunt Jean was another story. I was actually fine with her staying away. When she did visit, the conversation was primarily about her children and grandchildren and how wonderfully perfect they all were or how it was terrible that we couldn't find a "more qualified and American doctor" for mom. I finally had to tell her that if she couldn't stop her racist nonsense, then she had no reason to come by. Apparently, she took the hint, and her visits were also very few recently. Mom's only sister, Aunt Yvonne, lived one state over and didn't travel anymore, so they started calling each other a few times a week on the phone.

Even with mom's health in decline, Jack never visited more often than about every eight or ten days. He would bring mom the newspaper to read or flowers for her to display on the table next to her. They would talk for about thirty minutes at which point Jack would have someplace else to be. I could set my watch by their routine. What I really wanted was for my brother to offer to stay for more than half an hour. I wanted him to offer to pick up my grocery order or anything that would be the least bit helpful. I most likely would have turned him down, of course, because I'm stubborn, do it myself, kid of the 1980s and I don't need him or anyone else. But... I would have appreciated an offer all the same.

I didn't know how much time I would have left with her and with her birthday just a week away, I was planning something special. I was so excited because it kept my brain busy. I think deep in a dark corner, part of me knew that this could be one of the last times our entire family would be together as a unit. I wanted to make memories with her and not just *of* her. I felt quite certain that I was going to meet that challenge for her big day and what was even better was the fact she had no clue.

See? I said I love a good surprise; more so when I'm

the one giving it.

20

September 21

Mom's Eighty-third birthday

Being a stay-at-home caretaker has its advantages. What may you ask? Well, when your charge sleeps seventy-five percent of the day and all the other occupants are either at work or school, you find yourself with plenty of time to get one's home ready for a very large party.

After getting Mom up and enjoying her coffee for the day, I put the final cleaning touches on my home. By two o'clock this afternoon, my house would be filled with family and friends all here to celebrate Mrs. Evelyn Grace McIntire Northland on her big day and I wanted it to be perfect. I made quick work of Saturday breakfast for the family before returning to my party list one final time. I looked in my refrigerator and checked my list. Two plates of deviled eggs, four trays of various canapes, three types of finger sandwiches, and two cold dips; one savory, one sweet. Check. Cut fruit and vegetables for cold dips to be set out on a platter. Check. Meatballs, chicken skewers, and cocktail franks for the oven. Check. Moving to the pantry, I pulled out the blush-colored paper napkins I purchased and a brand-new tablecloth of the same color. Because I knew I wouldn't have enough stoneware plates, I also purchased white plastic dessert plates with gold trim. I pulled those off the shelf and placed them with everything else on my island. I spend the next thirty minutes counting forks, finding serving dishes, and vases, and setting up what will be the staging area for food. I also dusted off my old punch bowl that hadn't seen the light of day since Holly's baby shower for Jace.

I looked at the clock: eleven-thirty.

I sent Rhett out to pick up my order from the florist while Stacia and I got Mom ready.

"What do you think, Mom? You've got these nice gray slacks we can pull on…do you want the pink shirt or the yellow one?" I called to her from her walk-in closet.

"Pink…I'll just spill something on myself if I wear yellow…you know that…" she laughed until the coughing started. Mom was right; everything she owned in a yellow color had some sort of irremovable stain. I returned with a soft pink blouse and my daughter helped her get her arms into the holes. As Stacia brushed her grandmother's hair, Mom pointed back into the closet.

"Jera…you see that suit bag there?" she motioned.

"This one?" I pulled out the corner of the black

garment bag for Mom to confirm.

"Nope...the other one," and she continued to extend her arthritic finger.

I pull out a blue bag, "This one?"

"Yes."

"Okay...what about it, Mom?" I asked.

"Well...when I die...you bury me in those clothes," she said simply. "It's what I wore to your father's funeral."

I looked from Stacia to my mother, "Mom...we don't have to talk about this right now..."

"Well, when am I going to talk about it?" she chuckled. "It's just a fact of life...and you need to know what I want to be buried in."

I could see the conversation was upsetting Stacia and I had to switch it fast.

"Okay...we can do that," I grabbed a gray blazer quickly, "So, you want the jacket that matches those pants today or not?"

Mom shook her head, "No...it's not cool enough yet for all that."

"All done, Grandma," Stacia announced and handed Mom a mirror.

She smiled brightly, "Well...look at this old woman. I look pretty good...you did a nice job, sweetheart." She pulled Stacia's hand and my daughter leaned down to accept a kiss on the cheek.

After getting Mom settled back in her recliner, both Stacia and I hurried to ready ourselves for the day. As I returned back downstairs, Rhett and Remy walked in carrying four bouquets of flowers.

"Holy shit," I laughed. "Did you get the right order? I didn't buy all this."

"Well, these are yours," my husband handed off my

purchase, "And these are from someone named Gloria Steele…the others are from Remy."

"Gloria!?" Mom exclaimed from her chair. "I haven't seen her in years…"

Rhett placed Gloria's bouquet of pink lilies and white roses on the table next to Mom, "Here's the card, Mama E."

"Oh! That was so sweet of her…we used to work together, you know…we were charge nurses together," she said. My mom had worked hard her entire life and over her career at St. Vincent's Hospital, she had made a lot of friends; the closest being Gloria. Mom laid her head back and closed her eyes; she was tired again. I grabbed the small, crocheted blanket and put it over her lap. It was old and tattered and the brown yarn had started to unravel at one corner, but Mom loved the size and refused to part with it. I had something planned though that would hopefully take its place soon.

I finished laying out the warm food from the oven just as the first guests arrived a few minutes before two. I turned on some soft music that played through our surround sound system and we began greeting Mom's friends. As more people arrived, she was legitimately shocked at the reception. We held the party in what I would call open house style where people could come and go, have a bite to eat, and mingle. Mom was as ecstatic at seeing all of her people in one place. I walked around and assumed the role of barmaid and hostess, refilling drinks and chatting with everyone. Jack and Elaine were unusually on time and to my surprise, followed by his son JJ and family.

"JJ!" I exclaimed, genuinely happy to see my nephew.

Yeah, he's kind of an asshole like his father, but I do love my nephew.

"Hey Aunt Jera," he hugged me.

"Grandma's in the living room…right through here," I directed him.

"Thanks…is Val here yet?" he asked.

"Oh…I didn't know she was coming…I haven't seen her yet," I replied.

JJ glanced in his father's direction, "Dad didn't tell you?"

He looked a little irritated.

"Oh, no honey…but that's okay! "We have lots of room," I smiled brightly and patted him on both shoulders as he walked away. A few moments later, I heard my mother's distinct laughter as she saw her eldest grandson walk into her view. Jack's other two children, Valentine and Beckett arrived together thirty minutes later, and Mom again was overjoyed. By a quarter after three, my house was bursting with people. I was stealing a quiet moment to myself in the pantry when Rhett walked in with our niece.

"Aunt Jera," Val said.

"Hey, honey…how are you? How is school?" I hugged her.

"I'm good…I'll finish my graduate work in December," she replied.

"Congratulations! I'm sure your Dad is proud," I offered.

Hey…just because I have issues with my brother, does not mean I need to be unnecessarily rude to his kids.

Val shrugged, "Probably…but, I have a question for you…"

"Shoot."

"How long has Grandma been like this? I mean…she looks terrible," her expression was one of authentic concern, but mine was clearly one of confusion. Rhett frowned at me then glanced back at Valentine.

"Well…Val, she stopped any treatment for the cancer in the spring…the tumor just continues to spread. But we've seen a real change in her for a couple of months…why?" I asked.

"And Dad knew?" she blurted, frustrated.

"Yeah, Val…he knew. He knows everything that goes on…he comes to see her every ten days or so." I paused to read her face, "I'm guessing he didn't tell you anything…"

"No." She replied sharply and looked honestly hurt.

I reached out to give her a hug, "Oh Val…I'm sorry…I had no idea…"

"Aunt Jera…can you promise me something?"

"Sure…anything," I offered as I watched tears well in her eyes.

"Will you or Uncle Rhett call me if anything happens to Grandma? If she gets worse?" she asked quietly.

I looked at Rhett. Val had no idea the position she was putting either of us in with that simple request. Her father would be furious if he knew. But Valentine was twenty-five years old, and Jack couldn't possibly think he could control information between the family and his children forever.

Did he?

I nodded, "Of course sweetheart…I can do that."

"Thank you," she was trying to dry her eyes as Rhett handed her a napkin from a shelf. "I'm gonna go back out and sit with Grandma."

She turned and left.

I looked at Rhett in shock, "What the fuck was that?"

"No idea…Why wouldn't your brother tell his kids what's going on?" he replied, eyebrows raised.

I shook my head; I had no answer for him.

Around five o'clock, I shut the door on the last of our party guests. When I returned to the living room, Mom looked to be on cloud nine.

"Well, that was a hell of a party," I laughed.

"Oh, honey…that was wonderful…it was so nice to see everyone. And…nice to talk to other people besides your Aunt Jean. Ooo…that woman…sometimes. She can't shut up about how perfect her kids are all the time…like mine have been shit-eating servants their whole lives. I heard her yammering on in the corner to Elaine earlier…poor thing. If I could have gotten up and walked over there, I would have saved her from that mess," she complained.

"It's okay Mom…Elaine can hold her own," I said. I glanced over my shoulder and saw Stacia and Holly behind me, just out of Mom's sight. I knew what they had planned. "Hey, Mom…just one more thing before we can call it a real birthday…"

I moved so Mom could see her final surprise: A two-layer, chocolate birthday cake covered in pink frosting. Remy, Rhett, all the kids, Holly, and I sang the birthday song to her, and she blew out the large candle in the middle of the confection. I noticed through the smoke, Mom wiping away a single tear.

"Happy birthday, Mom, Grandma!" Everyone exclaimed.

Happy birthday, Mom…I thought to myself. A small voice whispered in my heart, and I knew that would be the last time I would say those words.

21

October 1

Life seems monotonous when your sole job is caring for someone. I don't mean that in an aggressive or even sour tone, I only mean to say that there isn't much variety when you watch someone sleep the majority of the day. But I find myself calmed by the serenity of it all. The rhythm of her breath and the soft sounds of her muted snore bring me peace. I am overjoyed when she mumbles, and I can catch a word or two from her dreams.

I watched her and I yearned to be a little girl again so I could climb into her lap and feel her soft hands caress my face and head. I want to nestle my face in her neck to breathe in her scent because I know time is the thief in the night and it will come to steal her away soon. I want to run my fingers through her hair and burn into my memory its texture. I want to be a little girl again so I can giggle at her funny faces and squeal at the top of my lungs "Mommy come play with me!!"

But that little girl no longer exists, and that mommy is frailer than cracked glass and I would not disturb whatever solace she is finding in her dreamland visions.

Through the front windows, I feel the autumn sunshine on my face as I lie on the sofa and watch her. Beegee has even noticed the change and refuses to leave her side for more than the time it takes her to eat or pee. Mom's hospice nurse, Amanda, came by today and said she would be visiting more often starting next week. They are also going to provide a bath aide, so I don't have to try and struggle alone to get her clean. It's a difficult task to maneuver a human, even one as small as Mom in a shower. She also suggested I consider allowing them to bring in a hospital bed and portable bedside commode. I told Amanda I would talk to Mom and get her thoughts first. I am humbled by the dedicated service these men and women provide to families like mine. It truly takes special people to perform the tasks they do and while I know that someone like Amanda would shrug off a barrage of compliments on the devotion she has, she and the others like her deserve more praise than I'm sure they get.

The house is sporadically empty as of late. High school football season is in full swing, so Rhett is usually late coming home most nights. Stacia's senior year has already been filled with loads of trips and activities. Between her school commitments, her new boyfriend, Josh, and her job, we don't see much of each other anymore, with maybe the exception of Sundays. Harrison has also been busy with his first semester of college. From what I can tell, he is enjoying his classes and the extra freedom his newly minted adulthood allows. He is also still working, so I don't see too much of him…actually less than I see Stacia.

I mean…I *think* my children still live here. At least, for now.

Jack should be over tomorrow. I figure I'll spend my time wisely and use our basement gym while he's here. I've been down there more often in the past couple of weeks since Rhett purchased a baby monitor with a camera for me. I hated to leave Mom on the main floor alone, but now I can see her from anywhere in the house. For now, she's still getting out of bed with assistance and sitting in her recliner most of the day. So, there are times during our day when she wants to try to use the toilet or return to her bedroom to sleep. The monitor keeps her from needing to yell out to find me and allows me to be a little more independent in the house.

I listen a little longer to the soft rumbling of her sleep. I close my own eyes to rest as my breath begins to synchronize with hers.

22

October 31

"Miss Evelyn, do me a favor and take as deep a breath as you can," Amanda's voice was commanding yet soothing. She placed the nebulizer face mask over Mom's mouth and nose as she gave her the instructions.

Mom was having a difficult time today with the constant hacking cough. Twice already it was bad enough that she yelped in pain and vomited. She just didn't have the strength to hold the handheld device in her mouth for more than a second or two and even if she did, she might fall asleep anyway. But Amanda was prepared for this development and made the change quickly and efficiently.

"Good job Miss Evelyn!" she cheered Mom on then turned her head to speak to me. "This will work out so much better…she can lay back and cat nap while this is on," she explained. "Have you thought about the bed and commode anymore?"

I nodded, "Yeah, I think we'll go ahead and do that...just let me know when they will bring everything, and I'll have Rhett and Harry take her bed down."

"Don't do that," she replied, "Normally, we like for the client to be set up in the living area, so they still feel like part of the family."

"I see...that makes sense, but when she's done, we should ask her...if that's alright?" I suggested.

Amanda smiled, "Of course! And if she doesn't want it out here, her room is big enough if they just move her bed over, we can get the hospital bed and air mattress in with no problem."

She turned her attention back to Mom, "Alright...I think you're about finished up." She took the mask off Mom's face, "Feel better?"

Mom nodded, "I don't want that bed in here... I don't want to be on display."

"That's perfectly fine... We will do whatever *you* want, alright?" She rubbed Mom's hand, "Now, I'm just going to get your vitals then I'll be out of your hair for today. I'll be back on Monday to do our med count, okay?" Amanda's smile was genuine and kind. She finished her tasks as she had explained and packed up her bag. I walked her to the door.

"Thank you so much for everything," I said.

"No thanks needed. I enjoy spending time with her...she is such a lovely woman. I'll be back on Monday...I'll get the bed and things ordered and they should deliver tomorrow...if anything changes with her, call the office, okay?" she replied.

I shut the door and returned to the living room;

Mom was finally asleep and breathing better. I put the receiver of the monitor on my hip and made my way out onto the deck. It was autumn in Missouri and the large maple trees in my backyard were on fire with fall color with a few leaves even making their way to the ground. I sat in a chair and stared into the empty lot behind my house that separated me from my neighbors. My mind must have shut my ears off because I never heard Rhett come outside. His hand touched my shoulder, and I was startled.

"Oh shit!" I exclaimed.

He chuckled, "Sorry about that."

"It's okay..." I smiled at him weakly as he took the seat next to me. "I didn't think you would be home until later."

"Well...I thought that I needed to spend some time with my wife," the corner of his mouth curled in a grin. "You know, I haven't really had a good conversation with her in a while."

I sighed, "I do know that..."

"So," he leaned back, "Let's talk..."

"About?"

"You," he stated flatly.

I shook my head, "Not much to tell..."

He stared at me.

I took another deep breath and stared back. We had a way of speaking without words.

"How's your mom today?" he asked softly.

"I thought we were talking about me," I countered with mild sarcasm.

Rhett raised an eyebrow, "Well, I've learned that to get a baseline on you, I have to know about her first."

Sigh number three.

"She's had two coughing...*fits*...today. Amanda left

a full mask to use with her nebulizer…it's nothing anyone will have to hold, so that should be easier. She's…tired and… weak…I'm changing her like six times a day."

He continued to study me. I leaned my head back on the chair and closed my eyes. I was also tired. It was a good thing that I had been hitting our little gym because every day was becoming a full-body workout as I lifted and transferred Mom from her wheelchair to the toilet to the bed to the recliner and back again. I could feel muscles I hadn't felt in years.

"Breakfast," Rhett said gently.

I didn't open my eyes, "Toast with avocado, coffee."

"Lunch," he continued.

I shook my head and he grunted.

"One day, Rhett…" I rolled my head and looked over at my husband.

His lips pursed before he spoke, "One day turns into five, Jera…your stress response isn't healthy…"

"I know…I promise, I'm watching it. I will eat a full dinner tonight, okay?" I really didn't like making him worry about me. I really *was* fine. I had come to understand my reaction to stress a long time ago; being a Marine wife does things to a person.

"Damn right you will," I heard the smile in his voice. "Because we are getting your favorite takeout for dinner."

An easy and automatic smile crossed my lips before I turned to look at him again, "Thin crust, everything pizza with extra cheese from Harper's?"

"Already made the order…" he stood up and kissed me on the top of my head.

My stomach was already growling.

I couldn't get Mom to eat anything that night. She seemed really out of herself and slept most of the evening in her chair. Holly brought the kids by to collect their Halloween candy from our house, and Mom, who usually loves seeing them in their costumes, barely opened her eyes. I knew after Holly left that Ashton and Jace would be my only trick-or-treaters since our driveway was nearly a quarter of a mile long, so I shut off my porch light. It took Rhett and I both to lift my mother from her wheelchair to the bed so I could roll her back and forth to change her brief and clean her up; a task that exhausted her even more. Afterward, I tucked her blankets around her, placed her water glass next to the bed, and turned out her lights. Beegee took up her nightly guard at the foot of the bed.

It had been a long day for all of us.

I went to my bathroom upstairs and turned on the shower. I waited until the room was filled with thick steam before I even stepped out of my leggings and t-shirt. The water was scorching as it bounced on my bare back and head. I stood there with the pounding cascade beating on me until I felt a cool breeze drifting by in my enclosed shower.

"How's the water?" Rhett's voice drifted from the fog.

"Good…" I groaned and shut the shower off. I opened the door, and he handed me my towel as he brushed his teeth.

"Tell you what," he swished water and then spit in the sink. "Go get dressed and I'll rub those knots out."

I yawned, "I think I need that…"

I dried quickly and then laid on my stomach awaiting my back rub. My heavy eyelids sank and before I could take my husband up on his offer, I was asleep.

23

November 5

The doorbell rang loudly making both Mom and Jack jump. The delivery driver left the small box on the stoop and was already pulling back down the drive when I opened the door. I was smiling when I returned to the living room.

"What is that?" Mom asked weakly with sunken eyes.

"This is your belated birthday gift," I replied, ripping open the clear tape that sealed the small white package. Jack eyed the box and even seemed to anticipate its contents. As I opened the flaps to peer inside, I could already tell it was more than I expected. I sat the open box in Mom's lap.

"Well, what is it?" she asked without looking.

"Mom, look in the box..." Jack urged her.

She slowly looked down into her lap and then began

to fumble with the item inside. My brother reached over and helped her free it from its package. It immediately unfolded and Mom's eyes widened. "Isn't that beautiful!"

The lap quilt was made from fifty, five inches by five-inch squares of pale pink colored fabric, that was trimmed with a second fabric made with a rose motif. But what made this blanket unique were the signatures that were embroidered with delicate gold thread on each block.

"I had all your friends and family sign a square at your party, Mom. See? There is Jack's signature…and here's mine," I pointed out two separate blocks.

Her eyes welled with tears, "Isn't that just beautiful…well, it seems too pretty to cover up with…"

"Well, you need to be able to enjoy it and it's washable…if you get something on it, don't worry," I replied as she tried to spread the small blanket on her lap. Jack reached over to assist her and tucked her in.

"Oh…I like this…" she smiled softly. While her smile was genuine, her eyes were dark and a little heavy. "I think I'll take a little nap now."

She leaned her head back and closed her eyes. Jack stayed next to her until he heard her snoring softly, then stood to leave.

"I'll be back next week," he whispered and motioned for me to walk him to the door. I put an old sweater on and called for Beegee to walk outside with us.

"When will a doctor be by to see her?" he asked.

Seriously. He never listens.

"No doctors, Jack…she's a hospice patient…the

nurse will be in tomorrow, then again on Monday," I replied.

"Surely, they have to work *under* a doctor's license…who is that person? Don't they see patients?" he countered.

"I'm sure they have a few on staff, but no…they don't see patients. She's terminal…there's nothing anyone can do," I tried to keep the frustration out of my voice.

"I know what she is!" he snapped.

I threw my hands up in surrender then turned to leave, "See ya next week, Jack."

"Wait…where are you going?" he asked.

"Back in my house…away from this argument," I retorted.

"What argument? We aren't arguing…"

"No? Well, then I'm going back in the house before you bite my head off again," I offered harshly.

"God, Jera…no one can talk to you anymore without you taking it as an insult or something," Jack rolled his eyes.

I sighed heavily, "If *someone* wanted to have a civilized conversation and actually *listen* to what I have to say…I'd be more than happy to oblige. But frankly, Jack…I'm exhausted, and I have no desire to waste what little energy I have, contending with you. I know you think it was a terrible decision for me to take over Mom's care…and I know you think I'm a complete idiot for not leaving her in that god-forsaken nursing home. And…you're still pissed off that I have her power of attorney and will be the executor of her estate… But Jack those are all *your* problems…not mine. Stop making the things you are angry over about me! Please just…let me take care of Mom in what little time she has left…we'll see you next week."

I had enough. I was done. I turned my back on him and walked back into the house.

24

November 8

Amanda stayed longer than usual today. Mom's condition continued to get a little worse every day and this morning, she refused to get out of bed. Amanda explained that it was perfectly normal for patients to get to a point where they just didn't have the energy to be transferred. She gave me a quick lesson on how to use a sheet underneath her to help slide Mom up in the bed and how I could use the adult diapers on her while she was bedfast. This was something I had to do no less than ten times during the day as my mother had practically lost all bladder and bowel control. I felt so grateful to have someone so kind and patient to help me take care of my mom. I honestly had no idea what I would do without her.

At lunchtime, I used the remote on the bed to lift Mom's head up for lunch. I sat a little wooden tray across her lap and pulled a chair up next to her.

"Hey, are you ready to eat? I made you potato soup," I said and placed a napkin over her chest.

"I don't know honey…" she shook her head.

"Mom…could you try?" I asked softly.

"I'm just not hungry," she explained. She looked from the soup to the spoon next to the bowl. "I guess I could have a bite or two…it looks good."

I smiled, "Okay…a bite or two." I fed her around five spoonful's of soup, making sure the bowl of the spoon contained broth, potato, and onion in every bite. On the sixth round, she began to shake her head.

"I'm done…no more," she said.

"Okay…how about a drink of water?" I asked and raised the straw to her lips. She took a small pull but was finished. I put the remaining food in the kitchen before returning to her room to settle her for a nap. I pulled her little pink lap quilt to her chin, and she snuggled down like a child. She looked so small…so frail. My always strong-as-steel mom was withering away before my eyes and there wasn't anything I could do to stop it. I desperately wanted to slow time down because I knew our hours together were being eroded away like mountains in the desert. And all I could do was watch it happen. I angered me. It saddened me. I also felt alone.

I had no one to help me with every task, every day. I felt like my life was on hold for her and I watched everyone else living theirs around me. I feel guilty for those thoughts. It was a privilege to be allowed to take care of her as she cared for me as a child. I could do this…I *had* been doing this.

I had no choice but to do this.

25

November 11

Jack sat next to Mom's bed for over an hour and watched her sleep. I had never seen my brother more uncomfortable or on edge. He sat, holding her hand with a furrowed brow, staring. It was almost as if he was willing her to wake. She had been sleeping almost nonstop for the past two days and had refused almost all food. Amanda had told me to watch for signs of pain, but outside of her typical MS muscle spasms, she didn't seem to be in any. I continued her normal regime of pain treatments until this morning when she was just too difficult to wake up, so I moved to the pain patches that had been ordered earlier in the week.

At Amanda's suggestion, and while Jack sat with mom, I called Remy to come home off the road. If she was slipping into unconsciousness, it may be his last opportunity to see her. And, if I hadn't called him, he would be angry that I hadn't let him help. He told me he was leaving right then and that he should arrive sometime around eight o'clock that night. I then took the opportunity to call other family members and make them aware of the situation. Aunt Leann said she and Uncle Chuck would be by in the next couple of days to visit and she offered to call Jean, which I accepted without hesitation. Aunt Patty sent her condolences and stated she would see if Chuck and Leann could bring her when they visited. Mom's sister, Yvonne, cried but said she knew her sister was in bad shape because of a dream she had had the night before. I kept my promise to Valentine, leaving a message to her that her grandmother had taken a turn and she was more than welcome to come to see her any time, day, or night. My final call was to my girl, Holly.

At around two that afternoon, Jack left stating he would come back in a couple of days. My immediate thoughts were about him and Remy being in the same house at the same time without the distraction of a party. But other worries invaded my mind, and that idea quickly became fleeting. I sat by her bedside until Harrison came in around three.

"Hey Mom…" he said softly.

I looked up, "Hi baby…how was class?"

He shrugged his shoulder as he gazed at his grandmother. I saw the pain in his face, and I immediately wanted that to go away.

"She's just sleeping, Harry…she opens her eyes if you talk to her," I offered.

He shook his head, "She needs to rest…I just…wanted to check on her…you…" he sighed. "Do you need anything, Mom?"

I smiled at my sweet boy, "No, son…I'm okay." I

checked the clock on the wall, "You better hurry…you work tonight, right?"

"Yeah…okay…" he replied looking at the time on his phone. "Is Stac home tonight?"

"I think so…if she's not out with Josh…why?" I asked.

He shook his head. "Just wondering," he bent down and hugged me, "Love you, Mom."

My heart broke into a million pieces. My son had always been his father's twin; especially in the way of matters of the heart. Over the years, Rhett had gotten better at expressing his more tender emotions with those closest to him, but Harrison was still young and tended to keep all of that to himself. My children were very close to their grandma, but that was to be expected as we lived in the same town, and Rhett and I made sure our families were always included and involved. It had been almost a year and a half since Mom had moved into our home and the kids were a large part of her enjoyment here. And while I never asked for my children to assist in her care, they volunteered over and over again. I realized at that moment that losing her would crush them both.

I left Mom's side as she rested and busied myself with planning dinner and doing some general cleaning around my house. Rhett and I ate together in the living room and were still there when Remy pulled in that evening. It was already too dark outside for him to set up his trailer, so I made sure the spare room had clean sheets and pillows. Once he was inside and settled, he helped me change Mom's wet briefs and pad and then get her cleaned up for the night. When we were done, he spoke to her for a moment and she opened her eyes, smiling weakly at his voice but her wakefulness was short lived, and she closed them again to sleep.

26

November 15

Dying is a dirty, stinking, hellscape for those that are caring for the ones transitioning. Even though she herself cared for the dying, if my mom were even a little bit conscience, she would be so embarrassed at the involuntary processes and smells that her surrendering body was producing. Don't get offended because I'm not mentioning any of this to shame her or anyone else. But, if you've never been witness to someone whose body is trying in vain to stop the process of shutting down, I want you to understand it's not what you see in the movies.

They don't just go to sleep.
They aren't always quiet.
The process isn't always quick and peaceful.

They have no control over their bladder or bowel and it's definitely not like cleaning up a baby. It's messy and because of the evil villain that is cancer, the smell alone will make you retch in the same trash can you put those adult diapers into; I've done it. Then there is the vomit and snot that ironically smells like what comes out of the other end. You constantly wash the same sheets and towels that you did the day before all in an effort to keep the person comfortable and clean. Their bodies are warped with pain that even the strongest narcotics don't always take away, which makes the entire hygienic process even harder.

Dying isn't always dignified.

"Jera!!" My mother cried out in pain one afternoon. I didn't need the baby monitor on my hip, I could hear her across the house.

"What's wrong, Mom?" I panted having just made a sprint from the guest bedroom into her suite. I watched as she struggled to pull herself over onto her side using the bed rail to assist.

Her eyes rolled into the back of her head, "I…can't…my wat-er."

Her voice was raspy and breathless. I gently grasped her thin shoulder and elbow and used my own strength to fully pull her onto her side. I placed the straw between her dry lips, and she sipped tiny little drinks. When she was finished, she released herself and panted as if she had run a marathon.

"Ohhhh!" she cried out.

Tears stung my eyes. I couldn't give her any more medication for pain for another two hours; she had all her frail body could handle.

"What's wrong momma? Do you need some pillows for your back?" I asked aloud.

"Ohhh! Damn it!" she hollered, crying angrily. I did my best to make her comfortable. I fluffed every pillow, created a backrest, and repositioned her head. As I gently pulled the thin blanket, she preferred up to her shoulders I rubbed the space between them softly. Her body seemed to relax for a moment, but her face was still drawn with pain.

Dying isn't always dignified.

And that is actually quite infuriating. How can a person that has spent their entire life caring for others deserve this kind of exit from life? It's not fair. Dying is not a happy ending, but someone so kind should get an expiration that isn't filled with more torment than they ever inflicted in the entirety of their life. I can't imagine very many people in which I would wish this sort of death upon. I don't know if I have that much apathy or hate in me.

I'm only comforted, if you can call it that, by the fact that I am sharing this entire experience with my husband and brother. They have been such a tremendous help over the last several days and help is something I have a difficult time asking for under normal circumstances. There will never be enough days in the rest of my life to thank them. I only wish that no one would have to witness the seeming dishonor cancer is inflicting on my beautiful mother.

The process of dying is the tragedy.

27

November 17

Mom had been unconscious for five days and we have been keeping a constant vigil by her bedside for six. Hospice was in twice this week and given her a bed bath, but Amanda stated yesterday that we might want to prepare ourselves for the inevitable. I am still confused by the word *prepare*.

How does one *prepare* for the death of someone you love?

It's not like I need to make sure she's packed enough underwear or has her dentures. It's not a vacation she's going on. How do I prepare? Should I make a cake or run to the liquor store to make sure we have enough beer? God knows I'm going to need a beer. You can't really mentally prepare yourself for death. It just comes. When my father was sick, we knew he was dying too, but his death was still a shock. Prepare. If you could, my family should be the most overly prepared people around because we knew this was coming for the better part of a year.

Prepare.

Maybe it should be said in a way that makes more sense. Like, "Brace yourself for impact into the steel reinforced concrete and brick wall that is debilitating grief." I just imagine myself on an airplane with elbows and knees locked as my brain stupidly thinks I can control the descent myself.

We knew it wouldn't be long. Days, hours, minutes, we had no idea, but we could feel death nearby; he was knocking on the door. While it had been only a week since she had taken in any food, she looked emaciated, a boney wasteland. Her skin had a dingy, grey tone and the coloring around her eyes was dark. Her lips were dry, and I did my best to keep them moistened with Chapstick and wet rags. She lay on her side with her body curled in a fetal position until she became restless and rolled onto her back in whimpering groans.

I felt numb. Maybe it's because of all the bracing I'd been doing, or it could be the cold, blustery November wind outside. I mean, I've done nothing today except stand at my front door and accept family into my home. Jack arrived around nine o'clock and took up a stoic position on Mom's right side. Aunt Leann came by for a few minutes just to see if I needed anything, but I didn't. Remy had been staying up at night with Mom, so I could get a little sleep. He didn't make it back into the house until eleven this morning.

Around eleven-forty-five, I was startled when Jack

yelled from Mom's room.

"Jera! Come here, quick!" he bellowed.

I scrambled to Mom's side to find her mouth making a gasping motion with her lips.

"Oh God," I mumbled. Amanda had told me what I might expect. "Remy!" I yelled but it was unwarranted as my twin was already at my side.

Mom gasped again.

"What's wrong with her!?" Jack demanded.

I remained as calm as I possibly could, "She's dying, Jack…this is death."

Jack closed his eyes.

Mom didn't gasp again but her breathing was shallow, and it sounded like she had rocks in her throat.

Death rattle.

Jack, Remy, and I stood around her bed, watching and listening. The minutes ticked by slowly as we held her hands and refused to allow her to go alone.

They say when you die, your life flashes before your eyes. What people don't know is the same thing happens when you watch a loved one die; their life with you runs in your mind like a movie on fast forward. You desperately reach out with your subconscious, grasping, clawing, trying to hold onto one of those moments and the feelings they produce until the film just suddenly stops.

The room fell silent.

None of us moved as we waited for her to breathe again but she was still. I took my fingers that were woven with hers and felt her wrist for a pulse.

She was gone.

I shook my head at my brothers as rivers of tears flowed freely from my eyes. Jack's head nodded over and over as he fought back his own grief and Remy stood quietly until I wrapped my arms around his neck, hugging him, allowing him the permission to release.

***

We waited for thirty minutes for the on-call hospice nurse to arrive and another forty-five for the funeral home to take Mom's body. We kept vigil at her bedside and said our goodbyes. Both Jack and Remy waited in the living room while they loaded her onto the gurney and laid the heavy, blue cover over her before strapping her down. The two mortuary men rolled her through the living room, out the front door, and easily off the porch, onto the sidewalk. Only after she was loaded and they made their way down the drive, Jack spoke.

"I guess we'll have to figure out her funeral," he said.

I shook my head, "Not really…Mom already had a plan in place…all we need to do is settle on dates and times."

"I see," he said as he looked down at his phone. He frowned and then looked back up at me. "How does Val already know about Mom?"

I blinked, "Because I told her."

"Why did you tell her?" his voice was shaking and hard.

I paused.

"Because she asked me too, Jack," I replied.

"When did you talk to Valentine?" he demanded.

"At Mom's party," I sighed. "She caught me in the

pantry…"

I didn't really want to tell him that his daughter was pretty upset with him for not telling her the truth about her grandmother's condition. What was the point now? The tension between us was already building and I didn't want another episode of my brothers exchanging blows in my front yard. Not now, not today.

"She's *my* daughter…I'll be the one telling her what is going on…don't talk to her," he growled through a clenched jaw.

"That's enough, Jack. Just…stop, will you?" Remy interjected hoarsely from the sofa. His eyes were bloodshot from expelled tears, and he looked defeated.

I heard a vehicle door shut and we all glanced out in time to see Rhett coming up the walk. Something shifted in Jack's face, and he thought better of pushing the issue further.

"Call me when the meeting at the funeral home is set," my brother said as Rhett walked in. He took his jacket off the sofa and walked out of the front door. I watched Jack leave but as soon as his car moved down my drive, my tired eyes shifted to my husband. Rhett didn't hesitate to wrap his strong arms around me, engulfing me in his chest. Sadness, anger, and worry released as I wept in his embrace.

28

November 18

Let me tell you about my mother…

Evelyn Grace McIntire Northland was born September 21, 1940, to Mrs. Mildred Erma Wilshire McIntire and Mr. Charles Alan McIntire at the family farm in Holbrook, Kansas. She was the eldest daughter of five children. She attended Saint Patrick of the Holy Cross church in Holbrook with her family and received her education until the age of fifteen at Holbrook Senior High School.

Why until fifteen, you ask? My uncle Gene, mom's older brother, was killed during the war in Korea in 1952. Mom decided to quit school a couple of years later to go to work in a local factory making airplane parts to help the family make ends meet. She worked there for five years before testing and passing the GED exam. In 1961, at twenty-one years old, she moved to

Kansas City, Missouri to attend school at the College of Saint Teresa, now called Avila University, where she studied nursing, receiving a three-year degree. She worked as a registered nurse in two separate hospitals in the area over several years. In 1969, while attending a co-worker's Christmas party, she met what she called "The most handsome green eyes she had ever seen in her adult life". The owner of those eyes was John William Northland, a thirty-five-year-old high school social studies teacher from St. Joseph.

From the moment they met, the pair were inseparable. They were together every spare moment, having all manner of crazy adventures. John liked to drag race and would take his hot rod and his new girl out every chance he got. After dating for two years, they were married on June 1, 1971, on the McIntire family farm in Holbrook, but made their home in the growing city of Michael Springs, Missouri. In March of 1972, Evelyn gave birth to a son, the couple named Jackson, after John's deceased father. In early August of 1977, Evelyn gave birth to twins, a boy they named Jeremy and a daughter named Jera. The Northland family was complete.

But what of Mom's career?

She never stopped working. As a matter of fact, when doctors told her it was time to begin her maternity leave, she politely didn't listen and continued working up to the day she went into labor with all three children. In 1980, Mom was made the head of nursing services at St. Vincent's hospital, working until she finally retired at the age of fifty-eight. Time is cruel though, and Mom only got to spend four years of her retirement with our dad, and three years after his death, she was diagnosed with Multiple Sclerosis.

She loved so many things in her life. As a child, she learned to crochet and after Dad passed, she took up the hobby again, creating everything from hats to mittens, to blankets, and she loved giving them away as gifts, "Just because". She loved her grandchildren. On the day that JJ was born, she scooped him up in her arms and said,

"I'm your grandma…do you want some cookies? Do you want some candy? We're going to have so much fun!"

This became a tradition for her, and she recited the same phrase to each child on their first day in this world. She meant those words. There was never a shortage of homemade cookies or treats at any time in her house and the kids always got the first pick at the largest and best-looking ones.

She loved baseball and especially her Kansas City Royals. She and Dad never missed attending at least one home game every year and in her first year of retirement, they began traveling to other states to see the boys in blue play. She could call plays and cuss them out better than most coaches. Next to watching her Royals play, she was never happier than when she attended her grandchildren's games. With the exception of Val, all of them played baseball or softball. Mom never missed an opportunity to see them play, even if it meant leaving one game in the last inning to make it across town to another. Rain or shine, she was always there.

Her favorite junk food snack was salty popcorn with a side of chocolate bar. She would eat a mouthful of the warm, buttery grain then break a piece of the bar off in the next bite. She loved Vodka tonics, Virginia Slim cigarettes, and Brussels sprouts. She giggled at a good, clean joke, and rolled over in belly laughs at a dirty one. She was the boss, but not bossy. She enjoyed steak but hated chicken. Her home was always as tidy as her appearance, she loved a good mystery novel, country music, and was a voting Democrat. But the most significant detail that anyone and everyone should know is that she supported and loved her children and grandchildren in all things.

***

"I think that's about it," Reverend Matthew said to the table and nodded to the dark-haired gentlemen at the end of the room. "Aaron, is there anything else you'll need from the family?"

"I believe we've covered everything today," the suited man gave us a consoling smile. "We'll just need the items and clothing she will be buried in…I believe you said you will bring them this afternoon?"

I nodded.

"In that case, the only thing to discuss would be payment," he pursed his lips. "Now, your mother did have a prepaid burial with us, so fortunately, the cost at this point is minimal."

Reverend Matthew stood, "This is where I make my exit…Jera, Jeremy, Jack. Thank you for allowing me the honor of presiding over your mother's service. I will see you all on Friday."

He left and the door made a soft click as it closed.

"What exactly is covered in her plan?" Jack asked, redirecting the conversation. He seemed a little skeptical and probably thought this was a bad investment decision.

Aaron smiled again softly, "Quite a lot, actually. Casket allowance, engraving of the headstone, makeup, hair, transportation, and grave digging are all paid in full. The only cost that isn't covered is for embalming. You'll also need to make arrangements for family flowers with your florist."

Jack raised his eyebrows, "Oh."

I removed my checkbook from my purse, "How much is due to you today?"

"Twelve hundred dollars. You can pay in full, or we can split the cost…"

"I'll pay in full today," I interjected.

Aaron smiled at me again and nodded, "I'll get you a receipt."

I wrote the check out to the Sacred Memory Funeral Home, pulled it from the book, and sat it on the table in front of me. My brothers and I waited in pregnant silence for the funeral director to return. I wondered to myself if Jack would say something stupid in this place. Anything. I almost wanted him to.

Wait. Why am I so angry right now?

In those quiet few moments, I searched my mind to find the answer. I was angry with Jack, as I have been most of my life. I realized though, until yesterday, there had been a larger-than-life dam that held back all my feelings of disappointment, resentment, and loathing I had for my eldest brother. That dam was named Evelyn. But she was gone. There was no guilt anymore for feeling the way I do about him and nothing except myself to keep *me* from speaking *my* mind. We were orphans now.

Wow. That hit hard. *Orphan.*

We would never receive another birthday phone call from either of our parents or get a card with fifty dollars tucked inside. We would never hear them say 'Merry Christmas' as they handed us cups of eggnog again. We wouldn't spend another Thanksgiving around a table with them or see the joy on Mom's face as she cooked that meal. It was her favorite holiday. She loved everything about it, planning and execution. She made meticulous notes about everything from grocery lists to what time everything should go in the oven. It was only in the last year or so that she allowed anyone to help captain the process.

My breath caught in my throat. Thanksgiving was in a week.

I shook back tears and the lump that had developed in my windpipe just as Aaron stepped into the room. He handed me a receipt and a business card.

"We will call you sometime on Thursday when she's ready…that way you can view her and let us know of any changes that should be made," he explained in his soothing voice. As I placed the items in my purse, my hand hit something hard.

"Oh! I…uh…I almost forgot," I said and took the small glass bottle out. "If it wouldn't be too much trouble…Mom…this was Mom's favorite color of nail polish. She's not wearing any right now," that lump was getting uncomfortably large.

Aaron smiled, taking the bottle from me, "Of course…that's not a problem at all."

He walked us back through the small hallway out of the meeting room and showed us to the door. The sharp November air caught me off guard and I gasped; thankfully, the lump disappeared.

"Let me know when we can view her," Jack said,

pulling his wool coat's collar up.

I nodded and he walked away. Remy and I watched him for a moment before heading toward his truck.

"Well, any place we need to go now?" my brother asked.

I shook my head.

He sighed, "You're gonna have to talk."

I eyed him and took a deep breath.

"About?" I asked.

"How you're doing…you okay?" his voice heavy with genuine concern.

I sighed, "Yeah…just thinking about what comes next."

Remy's truck roared to life, "What comes next? At this moment is a beer…maybe two. After that…well, you've got time to decide."

We arrived back at the house thirty minutes later to find Uncle Chuck, Aunt Leann, and Aunt Jean having coffee with Rhett in our dining room. I shook my coat off and placed it on a chair back before grabbing a cup for myself and my brother.

"How did it go?" Leann asked.

I nodded, taking a careful sip, "Good…everything's done…visitation will be Thursday at six, funeral at St. John's on Friday at 10…I just need to run by later with her clothes and wedding ring. How long have you all been waiting?"

"Oh, honey…not long," Chuck replied.

"Well, all the neighbors have brought stuff over…I've got plenty of food…is anyone hungry for lunch?" I asked. The general consensus was yes so, I pulled out meat and cheese trays, fruit trays, bags of chips, and loaves of bread. Here, in the Midwest, a family death equals food. I set everything on the kitchen island along with paper plates and napkins. We all fixed sandwiches and found our places again around the table. When we were full and finished, Leann and Rhett insisted on cleaning up, so I went to pull Mom's garment bag out of the closet; Aunt Jean followed me into the room.

"I don't believe I've been in here since your mother moved in," she commented.

"Oh?" I replied, distracted. I pulled the bag out of the closet and found a nice pair of black pumps to go with the ensemble. I laid both items on the hospital bed, then went into her bathroom to find her wedding band.

"When are they picking up the bed?" she asked.

I returned with the wide gold band around my own finger, "Sometime today."

"Hmm," she said.

I looked over the items assembled and realized I forgot earrings. I returned to the bathroom to find a nice pair I knew Mom liked.

"Jera, honey…I've been thinking about your Great-Grandma Betty's wedding rings…I think I'd like you to give those to me…and your Grandpa Jackson's watch," she said plainly.

I frowned at myself in the mirror. Did she just ask me for things that belonged to my dad? I poked my head out of the bathroom.

"Excuse me?"

"Well, those things belong to my family. I'd like to be able to pass them down," she replied as a matter of fact. I found the earrings I had been looking for, grabbed them quickly, and stepped back into the room.

"And they will be…to whom Mom saw fit to have them," I said in retort. Aunt Jean looked angry.

"Those didn't belong to your *mother*...they belonged to..."

"...To my father. Which, after he died, became my mother's property...since she was his heir," I interrupted boldly.

"I want those rings...and the watch!" she demanded.

"You're not getting them! They don't belong to you! If memory serves, *you* got a pair of diamond earrings when Great-Grandma Betty died...and *you* got Grandpa's house...so, I think you've gotten plenty. You're *not* going to take away *my* family's inheritance," I yelled. By now, our argument had gotten loud enough it had drawn a small crowd.

"Well, I don't think that's fair! What are *you* going to do with those things?" she demanded.

"It's none of your business what I'm going to do with them...and that's the point," I countered.

Her brow furrowed, "I don't like your disrespectful tone..."

"Disrespectful tone? What about *you*? It's pretty disgusting and disrespectful to demand trinkets that have never and will never belong to you when the owner hasn't been dead twenty-four hours!" I was on the brink of tears, but I would be damned if this woman would make me cry.

"Jeannette Marie! I can't believe you," Chuck's voice boomed.

"What?" she snapped.

"I believe it's time to go," he narrowed his eyes at her.

"Chuck..." she started to protest.

"I said now, old woman...or you'll walk!" he growled at his older sister. Aunt Jean turned on her heel and marched out of the room, cane in hand. Uncle Chuck looked at me, ashamed.

"I'm so sorry honey…I don't know what's gotten into her," he apologized. "We'll see you on Thursday."

I nodded and he left.

"What the hell was that?" Remy looked at me in astonishment and I glanced at Rhett. My husband raised his eyebrows and then turned, walking away.

29

November 21

Fall storm clouds swirled overhead in the darkening Missouri sky. It's not unusual for us to get torrents of rain this far into the year, but with the day being as clear and beautiful as it was, a storm wasn't exactly expected. I climbed into the passenger side of my Yukon and moved the seat back a bit; Mom had been the last person to ride in the seat months ago and I had already forgotten just how small she was. I smoothed out my navy-blue V-neck sweater and fastened my seat belt. Harrison and Stacia climbed in behind me as we waited for Rhett. Holly and the kids met us at the house and Remy offered to drive their group in his truck.

We arrived at the funeral home an hour before the public visitation, as was tradition for the private viewing for the family. We were greeted at the large colonial southern-style double doors by a woman with perfectly styled, short, dark hair, wearing a green pantsuit.

"Hello," her smile kind, "You must be Mrs. Northland's family...I'm Helen. Please, come in." The foyer was decorated with expensive-looking, sturdy furniture that sat on a rich, burgundy carpet. Helen directed us to a small white book sitting on a wooden podium.

"If you would like, you are welcome to sign the book. Have you been able to view her yet?" she asked.

I shook my head, "No...I think we'd like to do that now."

"Certainly. If you'll follow me, I'll take you into the chapel...she does look quite lovely," she replied. We followed Helen into a larger room that looked like a small church, with an open casket surrounded by copious amounts of vases and stands of flowers at the front where the pulpit should be.

My brother's and I picked a lovely pink metal bed for our mother's final rest. Under the recessed lighting of the chapel, it glittered a little like ocean diamonds. I was the first to arrive at her side. Helen was right; she looked lovely. Mom's eyes which had looked sunken and tired before seemed plump and natural. Her skin looked healthy and not pallid as it had in the past several weeks. Her nails were painted perfectly with her favorite polish and her hands lay naturally across her waist. She looked like she could just be sleeping. I moved over a little to allow Rhett to stand next to me.

"She looks good," he whispered in my ear, and I fought back a barrage of tears. The best I could do at that moment was to nod. He wrapped his arm around my shoulder, and we moved so Remy could look. When I turned, I noticed Jack and Elaine standing a few steps behind Remy and Holly. He nodded in my direction, and I returned the gesture.

Before long, the small chapel began to fill with friends and family from far and wide. The whole family began playing the part of host as we chatted with the visitors. Some people walked by to see my mother, some did not. Some people that spoke to me, giving their condolences, I wouldn't have been able to pick their name out of a hat. I spoke with cousins I had not heard from in years. There were coworkers of my mother *and* father's that came to pay their respects, telling us stories of the perfectly matched couple and all their shared memories. What I did not expect were the familiar faces of the past few months making an appearance.

As I spoke with an older family friend, someone laid their hand softly on my back. I turned to find mom's nurse, Amanda, standing behind me. The moment I saw her, I burst into tears. She threw her arms around me in a warm embrace.

"Oh, Jera," she said softly, "I am so sorry for your loss. She was an amazing woman…I am so glad I got to know her."

I pulled away, wiping my tears, "Thank you so much…you just don't know how much it means to me that you're here."

"Well, I'll be honest, I don't usually go to the services…but your mom…was special. I guess I just felt a kinship with her because of her profession," Amanda smiled brightly.

We spoke for a few more moments and she went to see my mother. I was so grateful for everything she had done to take care of mom; that would never be forgotten. I looked over the crowd that had gathered and realized that Mom had touched all of these people in some way throughout her life. It was a heavy thought, but it made me feel proud. I was happy they knew her. As the first hours began to wind down, I also realized there were no classless incidents involving anyone's bad attitude or inflated sense of privilege tonight.

I call that a win.

The entire event, start to finish, lasted three hours and was incredibly overwhelming, to say the least. By the time we pulled back onto our driveway, I felt as though I had just worked a three-day shift. I was exhausted and my mind was shut down. I didn't want to talk to another soul or engage with anyone else for the rest of the night. I needed quiet solace. Luckily, it was as if everyone in that truck could read my thoughts because none of us spoke as we entered the house. I made my way upstairs to my bedroom, dressed for bed, then collapsed into sleep.

30

November 22

We were lucky that the cold rain let up.

Actually, my mother would have been laughing if it hadn't. She would have found it absolutely hysterical that we dressed up for her, only to have to deal with a mini monsoon. It's like I could hear her laughing:

"Dummies…standing out in that weather getting your fool heads rained on."

She always did have a twisted sense of humor.

I was up early for coffee when I heard my brother open the door to the spare bedroom. His shuffling stride made a swishing sound on the carpeted hallway.

"Morning," he yawned.

"Morning," I replied, sipping the skunky heaven in my cup. "You hungry?"

Remy shook his head, "Nah…I'm good." He

186

poured himself a cup of coffee and then sat at the dining room table across from me.

"What's on your mind?" he asked.

I shook my head curtly.

"Jer…"

I closed my eyes. I really wasn't trying to be rude, but I just didn't think my eyes could handle any more tears. I didn't want to talk about it or anything else. Mom was dead; that's all she wrote. I wanted to just get this day over with and ready myself for the depression that would come. I had taken care of Mom in some capacity for the past eighteen years and the last eighteen months was daily care. She and I were a team of sorts; I don't think anyone understood that. I felt like I had lost a limb; that a part of me was gone.

I squeezed my eyes tighter. Don't let them fall.

My brother's hand was warm on my own.

"Jera," he whispered, "I know you miss her…and I know how hard this is for you. I'm sorry."

Opening my eyes, I stared blankly at my twin. Sorry? "Why?" I blinked.

"Because out of everyone, this burden sat on your shoulder's the heaviest. Maybe I should have been around more…even if you protested." He raised his dark eyebrows at me, "You know you would've."

"Yeah," I smiled.

"I'm sorry you had to do this alone," Remy stated softly.

I squeezed my brother's hand, "I wasn't alone…You, Rhett, Holly…even the kids…I had you all with me. I appreciate that."

"Here…" he said, sliding an envelope at me.

"What is this?" I wrinkled my nose, reaching for the packet.

"My share of the expenses…I'm betting Jack won't even offer. But it's not fair that you shoulder that burden too," he replied.

I opened the envelope and counted six, one-hundred-dollar bills.

"Rem…"

He shook his head, smiling, "Don't even try…done deal. Take the money, dummy."

We sat in shared silence and sipped coffee. The sun began to peek through the storm clouds and beams of light pushed through the back sliding door. I began to hear footsteps above our heads as the rest of the house began to wake. As Harrison and Stacia made their way to the kitchen to grab some quick breakfast, I rinsed my cup and placed it in the dishwasher. I made my way back upstairs to ready myself for the day.

Whatever this day was going to be.

Numb is a good word to describe the cacophony of emotions that swirls about in a person's mind and overwhelms them until they are no longer separate responses anymore but just one mutable feeling. Numb is what I felt right now. I knew it would be fleeting though as I applied the last swipe of lipstick to my mouth. I stared hard into that mirror trying to convince the reflection that she was strong enough to keep her shit together one last day.

I don't believe she bought it either.

"Hey…you about ready?" Rhett's voice sounded behind me.

I inhaled, "Yeah…ready as I'll ever be."

I gave myself one last look before meeting my husband at our bedroom door. To be honest, it was kind of weird seeing myself in something that wasn't almost entirely made of spandex or denim. In the past year and a half, my wardrobe was made up of yoga pants, tee shirts, hoodies, and jeans. Today was different. Today I would dress up for her. I wore my black pants suit, matching it with a nice pale pink knit top. I donned the pearl earrings I received from Mom as a gift when Rhett and I were married and my watch, then slipped into my black Cole Haan pumps.

I clean up pretty damn well.

We arrived at St. John's Episcopal Church at a quarter after nine. Reverend Matthew greeted us at the door and escorted us to a side room where other family members were being staged. Rhett and I said our cordial greetings to those who were already waiting and made small talk. It was about five minutes before the service was to begin when Aaron entered the room.

"Good morning, everyone. On behalf of Sacred Memory, I want to thank you for allowing us to be your guide through this difficult time," he paused. "Right now, we're going to have the family line up so you may enter the sanctuary. We will start with the eldest child..."

I glanced over at Jack as he and Elaine began the line followed by Remy, then myself and Rhett. Suddenly, I had an overwhelming feeling that this lineup wasn't right...there was something or someone missing. It was almost a desperate and nagging feeling that I couldn't shake. I turned to my husband, who mistook my need for his attention as desperation.

"What's wrong?" he whispered hoarsely.

"Where is Holly?" I asked.

Rhett frowned, "I don't know...probably already sitting down."

"No...she needs to be here...now," my voice was shockingly demanding.

What the hell is wrong with me?

"Okay…okay, we'll find her," he replied turning to talk to Harrison. Aaron continued to line up the family members as I waited impatiently for my son to return with Holly. Once in the same room, she looked worried.

"Hey…what's wrong? Everything okay?" she asked, searching my face.

I shook my head, "No…something is nagging at me…you need to be in this line with us."

Holly looked at the row of people.

"Sweetie," she whispered, "This is family…"

"No Hol…you need to be right here," I stated firmly and pointed directly between Remy and me. "Just…trust me…I don't know why, but something is screaming in my head that you need to be here."

She looked from Remy back to me again.

"You heard her," my brother shrugged. Holly stepped in line and my wave of anxiety ceased.

Weird.

"Alright, looks like that is everyone," Aaron declared. "We'll start filing in now."

We made our way down the aisle while a piano rendition of *Ave Maria* by Shubert played while the entire congregation respectfully stood. Once we were all sat in our pews, the music faded and Reverend Matthew began, "I am the Resurrection and I am Life, says the Lord. Whoever has faith in me shall have life, even though he die. And everyone who has life, and has committed himself to me in faith, shall not die forever…"

I have to admit here that this is a common funeral rite and I tend to zone out. My family has never had religion forced upon us, but it's something that Mom kept close to her heart. She loved going to services when she could and I think she secretly wished she could have been more involved in church activities, but her career took precedence. I wanted to pay more attention to the ritual of it all today, but I knew I had to keep my mind busy, or I would break. I looked over my shoulder, to my right, and watched JJ looking stoically at Reverend Matthew. Valentine wiped tears from her eyes as Beckett tried his best to keep his from falling. I craned my neck a little to find my children but when I did, Rhett squeezed my hand. He knew what I was doing, and he was right to stop me; if I had seen the shape my kids were probably in, I would have melted into a sobbing mess.

As it were, I glanced left and watched Remy's wet face, blanketed with tears. It was then that a tiny movement diverted my eyes and had I not been at my mother's funeral, I would have audibly gasped. Holly, who was sitting directly next to me, reached over and took Remy's hand. Now, that in and of itself wasn't a big shocker; Holly was the kindest person I knew, and she and Remy had been friends for years. But it was the way that Remy laced his fingers into hers that set my brain on fire. I couldn't help but smile. This was an intervention on a cosmic level, I just knew it. I understood why Holly had to be in that line; it had nothing to do with me, but everything to do with Mom making sure my brother found his soul mate.

Well played, ma'am.

I realized suddenly that the reading of the Gospel was over, and the congregation was being seated again as Reverend Matthew returned to the pulpit.

"As we gather today to celebrate the life of Evelyn Northland, we remember a woman of service and dedication. From her humble beginnings in a small Kansas town, all through her life, Evelyn served everyone she met, in some way. At the age of fifteen, her family struggled to make ends meet, so she went to work in a factory to offer what little help to them she could. Years later, she became a nurse and served the people she cared for in hospitals and clinics. But, as her family will tell you, she served her children and grandchildren the most. They got the lion's share of her time, her grace, and her love."

It was at this point that I wasn't able to hold back the tears any longer and I let them come. I let all the sadness and grief envelop me and allowed every cell of my being to feel it. Rivers I could no longer hold back poured down my face and dripped off my chin. The cheap, thin sheets of tissue were no match for my tears; I went through six of them within minutes. Reverend Matthew continued to eulogize my mother and talk about how much she loved being a mother and grandmother. He spoke of her love of baseball and her sharp wit. By the end of his lovely speech, there wasn't a dry eye nor a laugh left un-giggled.

The family followed my mother's casket out of the church and watched over her as the six pallbearers, all her nephews, lifted her into the hearse. Once everyone was lined up again in their vehicles, we followed the black leader to Mom's final resting place.

A thick royal blue tent was set up around the hole

that had been dug just that morning and offered us a small piece of refuge from the chaotic weather of the day. The sun peeked through shifting gray clouds that spat random drops of giant rain. I again heard mom laughing; she would think this was utter idiocy to stand over her in this weather. But there we were, all three of her children, standing side by side.

I knew this moment would never happen again.

I looked to my far left again and found Jack's eyes wet with tears as Elaine rubbed his hand. I saw Remy trying to remain unflappable, but I knew it was a show; he clung to Holly's hand, even pulling it closer to himself for comfort. I looked to my immediate right and ran right into the steely, tear-filled eyes of my husband.

That wasn't what I wanted to see, and the tears returned.

He wrapped his arms around me, pulling me tightly against him. He kissed my temple but never spoke; he didn't have to. He knew my pain because I think he felt it also. Everyone gathered as close as possible under the shelter as the charming voice of John Denver sang *Take Me Home, Country Roads* from somewhere overhead. When it was time and after the reverend had concentrated my mother to her rest, I followed Jack and Remy in picking a pale pink rose from a bucket and laying it on her casket.

"I love you, momma. I'll miss you every day…give Dad a kiss for me," I whispered my final goodbye, tears streaming off my chin.

After several minutes of visiting with friends and family that attended the graveside services, Rhett, the kids, and I began walking back to the truck. I was about halfway across a small empty piece of the cemetery when I heard someone calling my name from behind. I turned to see Jack making his way over.

"What does he want?" Rhett said quietly frustrated.

I shrugged and we waited.

"Hey…uhm," Jack looked at Rhett, "Can I have a quick word with Jera, Rhett?"

Rhett looked at me for approval. I nodded and he walked around to the driver's side of the truck, and got inside, but didn't shut the door. I turned back to my brother.

He looked down to the ground, then back at me, "I…uh…I just wanted to say thank you for taking good care of her…"

His voice broke and he coughed.

"I know it was hard…and…well, just… thank you."

I almost couldn't move so I did the only thing my brain immediately thought, and I hugged him.

"I would do it again, a million times over," I whispered. My brother held me close for a moment longer before he released me. I heard him sniffle as he nodded to me and turned, walking away. I watched him approach Elaine before the pair went to their own car. As I did, Remy and Holly were making their way toward me, still, hand in hand. I grinned at them as they came closer to me.

"So…" Holly smiled at me, doing her damn best to divert my attention, "Lunch at the church, right?"

"Uh-huh," I smirked.

"What was that about?" Remy asked, shoving a thumb in Jack's direction.

I shook my head, "I don't know…"

31

November 30

Thanksgiving came and went as quickly and as quietly as I had hoped. It was our first holiday since Mom's passing and I really didn't have the festive spirit in me at the moment. Rhett's mom was exceptionally gracious, making all of the food and hosting not only our family, but also Remy, Holly, and the kids.

Remy and Holly.

It had only been a little over a week since the funeral, but they had become inseparable. And it could've been because we had all been friends for so many years, but they seemed to skip all the awkwardness of a new relationship and get right to the good stuff. If someone from the outside didn't know better, they would have guessed the pair had been together for years, not a week. They were in tune with each other so perfectly that when she moves, he moves. It's also nice to see Remy smile a genuine grin again. He is truly happy.

I sat in the middle of my Mom's closet floor searching through financial paperwork when my brother rolled in this morning.

"Hey…" he called from the closet door.

I startled a bit, "Oh, hey…you heading out?"

"Yeah…I've got to finish up this contract…runs until Christmas. Then, I'm home," he replied.

"That's nice," I flipped through the manila folder I held, clearly distracted.

He paused.

"Did you hear what I said?" The smirk was evident in his voice.

I turned around more to get a better look at him, "Yeah…leaving today…finish the contract, then you'll be back."

He smiled, shaking his head, "No, Jer…I'll be *home*…for good."

"Really?!" I squealed with excitement and my head spun. I was absolutely overjoyed that he was planning to stay. Jumping up, I threw my arms around his neck, "This wouldn't have anything to do with a certain special someone, would it?"

I couldn't help but tease him a little.

He laughed heartily, "Well if I said it didn't, you'd call me a liar."

"One hundred percent," I smiled. "But I am happy for you Rem…"

"I know. Man, it's so weird though, you know? I mean, I was in love with Hol when we were in high school…hell, I don't know that I still didn't have a little crush on her when Katie and I got married…but you know, life…" he explained.

I nodded.

"I don't know what it is…I just sat there that day, knowing Mom was in that box…that we'd never see her again…and then…something just clicked. After she took my hand…something told me not to let her go…" My brother's eyes were misty, and I was in complete shock. Remy had never talked about any kind of emotions. Ever. I knew admitting anything like this to me meant something serious, but I also wanted to believe that Mom played a role in their new relationship and *that* idea made me happy.

Remy looked at my hands, "What'dya got there?"

"Oh, Mom's banking information…retirement…life insurance…and a couple of certificates of deposit," I replied.

"Huh," he mused. "I didn't know she had all that…how much does it come to?"

"That's the thing…Rem, if I'm reading this right, we'll each get around one-hundred-thousand dollars," I estimated.

Remy's eyes went wide, "You can't be serious…are you sure?"

He looked over my shoulder as I opened the folder again. I let my brother thumb through the documents watching his face drop more with astonishment.

"Holy shit," he whispered under his breath. "But wait. Won't this go to probate court?"

"I don't think so," I disagreed. "Look…she has us as beneficiaries on everything…even the CDs…and this is a trust. I think it will just transfer."

"I had no idea," Remy replied.

I shook my head, "Me either…but, it'll have to wait until I get copies of the death certificates anyway." I closed the folder.

"Well, let me know if you need anything before I

get back," he hugged me then looked me directly in the eyes, "I mean it."

I smiled, "I will…promise."

I continued to rifle through the different boxes and containers that lined the inside of my Mom's closet. The more I looked, the more treasures I found. In the far corner, I opened a large, black plastic box with RUBBERMAID stamped across its lid. I peered inside to find three white books stacked neatly together on one end and a smaller, square box on the other. I picked up one of the books and opened it. The front page read:

Baby's First Five Years

This book belongs to: Jackson Robert Northland

Oh my God; Jack's baby book, which meant the other two belonged to me and Remy. I found mine, the bottom of the three; probably because I was technically the youngest and opened it. The pages were yellowed slightly from age, but the rose gold trim looked brand new. I recognized Mom's handwriting immediately and traced it with my finger as I read my name out loud.

Jera Elizabeth Northland

Tears fell from my eyes. It was an overwhelming thought to know this would be as close as I would ever get to her again. I closed my eyes to remember what her hands felt like in mine. I thought hard about the last time I saw her sign her name on a check, just so I could remember how she held the pen. By the time I opened my eyes, my face was covered in tears and snot. I looked around the closet for something to wipe my face but instead of an old sock, I found Rhett's hand holding a box of tissues.

"Oh! I didn't know you were there," I said, a little embarrassed at my state. He handed me the box and after I cleaned my face, Rhett helped me to my feet. I wiped a lone escaped tear from my face.

"Sorry about that," I whispered.

He frowned at me before wrapping me in the tightest hug I can ever remember having. He kissed the crown of my head before talking softly in my ear, "This is going to be hard…but I swear you won't do it alone."

He held me for a long time while I sobbed, "God Rhett, I miss her so much."

I cried in his chest so long and so hard that my head and throat throbbed with pain. People will tell you that losing any parent is difficult and that everyone processes that grief in a different way and at a different rate. When my dad died, I grieved for him, I missed him; I still do. But losing her… was so much harder; I lost my Mom, my friend, and my daily companion. *I felt lost.* After I was able to regain my delicate composure, I wiped my face once more and looked up at my husband.

"Better?" he asked.

I nodded; I did feel a little better.

I turned to look at her room, "I just don't know where to start or what to do."

Rhett paused in thought for a long moment before he spoke.

"Do you have what you need, as far as her paperwork is concerned?" he asked.

I nodded.

"Then, we're going to shut this door for another week. If you feel up to it then, we'll start small…we don't need to rush. One box at a time," he smiled at me.

He was right. There wasn't a need to clear the room immediately. Everything could stay the way it was for a little while longer as I took time to sort through her possessions and my feelings. Other things were pressing, and I refused to stress myself out; everything would hold a little bit longer.

Well…at least that's the plan.

32

December 6

We woke this morning to three inches of soft, white snow covering the ground. Which is to say that it was a sufficient amount to completely create a beautiful clean canvas over my yard. I'm not one for cold weather, but I have to admit, I do love a good snow, especially on a weekend. I could hear Rhett making noise in the kitchen as I took my robe off the hook behind the door and made my way downstairs.

Before I hit the bottom, the smell of bacon and pancakes wafting from the kitchen made my stomach growl. I shuffled to the island and watched my husband work his magic.

"Good morning!" he said brightly.

"Morning..." I yawned.

"Morning, Mom!" Stacia chirped as she came out of the pantry. "You want coffee?"

I eyed my family before a "Yes," was released from my mouth.

Rhett chuckled, "Why are you suspicious?"

"What's going on?"

I was suspicious.

"The kids and I had an idea…since it's Saturday and everyone is home this morning, we thought we might have some breakfast and decorate for Christmas," he handed me a plate of food.

Christmas. I hadn't actually thought about another holiday let alone decorating for one. I knew what they were trying to do, and I did appreciate them for it. I had been a bawling, depressed mess for two weeks now and it wasn't fair to them or myself. Not to mention, Mom would be upset with me if she knew how I was handling everything. I gave my husband a small smile and accepted the offer.

"Sounds good," I replied.

While Harrison and Rhett carried up boxes of decorations from the basement, Stacia and I sat in the living room and sorted it all. By noon, we had our eight-foot artificial tree erected and dripping with sparkle and lights. We hung greenery around every window, doorway, and down the banister. I tucked faux holly in every nook and cranny while the kids hung stockings along the mantel. We laughed and we giggled, and I even convinced my son to play Christmas music on the surround sound system, against his better judgment, of course. After we finished, it looked like the North Pole exploded all over my house; but it didn't matter, I loved it. By three o'clock, both kids were heading out for work, and I sat snuggled against my husband with a cup of tea.

I realized then that this was the first time in almost two years that I didn't have anything to do on a Saturday. Nothing at all. Until that moment, I had been running from one place to another or doing something for someone else; and not just my mother. Two years ago, there was football, basketball, track meets, dances, or piano lessons; always something. Now, I sat quietly leaning against the love of my life, sipping my favorite cinnamon tea, and admiring our spectacular abilities as a decorating team. I felt…at peace. But it was more than that, I felt my grief for the loss of my mother take a different hold on my heart; one that wouldn't haunt me every minute of every day. I felt ready to come to terms with those emotions and accept that they would now always be a part of who I am. Would I still cry? Absolutely. Would I miss her? Every second of my existence.

But it was time to get shit done.

33

December 10

First order of business: Finishing my Mom's business.

After getting Rhett and Stacia out of the door, I sat at my dining room table with my mother's manila folder open, its contents sorted by category and company. Next to it, I had a large envelope with a ten-count of her death certificates at the ready. I remember my mother doing the same thing when Dad died, so I wasn't going into this blind, but I also knew it could take a while. I made my first call to her life insurance agency.

By around noon, I had wrapped up as much as I could with everyone being as kind as possible and offering their deepest condolences. Some of them gave me more homework to do while others just stated I would receive more paperwork in the mail. I then picked up her credit card bill as canceling the card would be the last item for today. I jumped through the automated hoops until the program instructed me to press zero for a live agent.

I pressed zero and waited for the line to connect.

"Thank you for calling…my name is Chris…how can I help?" Chris offered drolly.

"Hello, Chris. My name is Jera McKay…my mother, Evelyn Northland is a customer of yours…she has passed away and I'm looking to cancel her card," I explained.

I heard Chris clicking on his keyboard.

"I'm sorry…do you have the card?" he asked.

"I do," I replied and read the account number to him.

Silence.

"What was your name, ma'am?"

"Jera McKay…"

He paused again, "Ma'am, I'm not showing you as an authorized user on this card…"

"That's because I'm not. I'm calling to get the process started in canceling this card…my mother has passed away," I explained again.

"Your mother is Ms. Northland?" he reiterated.

"Yes," I said emphatically; now we're getting somewhere.

More noise on the keyboard.

"Unfortunately, an authorized user will need to call in for any changes made to the card," Chris explained.

I was getting frustrated, "Fine…can you tell me who one of those are?"

Again, keyboard clatter.

"I'm not showing any authorized users on this card," he replied.

I paused, "Then, how do I get this card shut down?"

"Ma'am, an authorized user will need to be added and then that person can either use the card or cancel the card," he said, his tone getting huffy.

Was this guy serious?

I started laughing, "So, Chris, what you're telling me is that my *dead* mother will need to call into your center and put me on the card as an authorized user so I can call you back and tell you she's *DEAD* and cancel the card?"

I was legitimately almost in belly rolls I was laughing so hard. Chris, however, was very quiet as, I assume, he processed the logic.

"Ma'am, I'm not sure what's funny," he began.

I laughed louder.

"Oh my God…is there a supervisor I can speak with?" I asked.

Chris sighed, clearly frustrated, "No, ma'am…they will tell you the same thing…"

"Oh, I hope they do…" I interrupted.

"Ma'am…"

"No, Chris…just no. She's dead…you do understand what that means, right?" My sarcasm was starting to seep out.

"Yes, ma'am…I understand what dead is…"

"Good! Because I'm going to make this very clear: She. Is. Dead. As in, not living, not able to come to the phone. She will *not* be able to add me as a user. So, this is what I propose…there is no balance on this card…so, there is no reason for us to speak again. I need you to give me a fax number or an email where I can send her death certificate… at that point if you or the company still need to speak with her…maybe we can find you the phone number to a good psychic," I said sharply. Chris complied with my request, and I gave him a cordial goodbye as I hung up the phone.

I sat silently for a moment contemplating my next call-- to Jack.

I hadn't spoken to my brother since the graveside services; not even at the luncheon afterward. I knew he wasn't avoiding me or I, him, we just didn't have anything in common anymore. The only tie that bound us was gone and I honestly was okay with it, as I'm sure he was. Realistically, we were never that close to begin with, even as children. To me, he was always the older brother that was always living another life with no interest in me or mine in it. I don't say that to be hateful or even to garner sympathy, it's just real life. I took a deep breath and dialed his number.

It took four rings before he picked up as I'm sure he contemplated if he would answer at all.

I mean, that's what *I* would have done.

"Hello?" he said.

"Hey, Jack…it's Jera. I'm not interrupting anything, am I?" I did my best to be polite.

He cleared his throat, "Uh, no…no, you're good. What's up?"

"I just wanted to let you know that I've been taking care of all the loose ends today…you're going to get some paperwork in a few days from Mom's financial planner for your part of her retirement…and Dogwood Bank will need you to come in to sign some things for the certificates of deposit," I explained.

"Ok. I'll look for it," he said shortly then paused, "What about her jewelry?"

He caught me off guard and I was quiet for a

moment.

"What about it?"

"When are we going to get it sold?" he insisted.

"Sold? I'm not sure there'll be anything left to sell…" I replied.

"Why?" he hissed. "Nobody wants it anyway…and a third of it belongs to me."

Like hell.

"You think so? *Nobody* will want it? Well, I'll tell you something, Jack…when I've decided to sort through it, I'll let you know what you can have. But let's be clear…Valentine and Stacia will get a share of their grandmother's possessions…Mom already made sure of that," I charged.

"What do you mean? Mom made sure of what?" he growled.

"Meaning…Mom has already made her wishes very clear on her possessions…and I'll not go against it," I replied.

"What do…." he started before I cut him off.

"I have pictures…of her things… she's written on the back who it belongs to, the date, and her signature…by the way…all of her jewelry is going to her girls…Me, Valentine, and Stacia…so, like I said…I'll let you know what you can have," I spat.

Jack was silent; so much so that I thought he hung up.

"Fine," he said quietly, and we sat together in silence for another moment.

"Look, Jack…I know you think that Mom didn't have her shit together later in life…but she did, and she was very specific. I don't wanna fight with you about this…I'm done with it…just let me get this finished for her and you can forget you have a sister!"

I hung up.

The one thing I miss from my youth is the ability to slam a receiver down. Even though it really didn't cause any pain to the person on the other end, there was just something wholly satisfying about being able to hang up a phone forcefully. The soft *click* of a cell phone just didn't have the same sort of effect. The same goes for our cordless landline; truly disappointing.

I sat for a long time on the sofa looking out of the window, reflecting on the day so far. It was only one o'clock and the score was already three to two, helpful people versus morons. I know, it wasn't very kind of me to lump my brother on the moron team, but it is what it is. I continued to think about how life would be so much different now with Jack and a tiny part of me felt a little sad. The one thing that our mother always wanted is the one thing we still can't pull off, but believe me, I tried. I would and *have* done anything for her; including being around a person who, let's be honest, has an abusive personality, but I'm not pulling his weight anymore. It's complete nonsense to try.

Instead of sitting and wallowing in what ifs and maybes, I decided to live life today. I have been the queen of online shopping as of late and this would be the first time in a couple of years that I would have the opportunity to visit actual stores to shop for Christmas; alone and at my own pace. It seemed like a foreign but refreshing change.

Man, was I ready for it.

34

December 24

Tonight, the house was warm with lights and candles. I spent the better part of the day baking cookies with Stacia and her boyfriend, Josh with Beegee bouncing at our feet begging for scraps. I was just getting ready to sit down with a cup of tea when I heard the familiar roar of a truck pulling into the drive as the pooch lying at my side began to bark wildly: Remy was home. It was a flash in my mind as I remembered this time it was for good. Harrison opened the door for his uncle, and I felt the large draft of cold air rush through the house.

"Hey Mom, look outside!" My son called out.

I turned in my seat on the sofa, pulling back the curtain; it was snowing. My heart lifted a little when I saw the flakes floating in the wind. I've never been one for cold, snow, or ice, but on Christmas, I'd take it as it only added to the spirit of the season, and this year, I needed all the help I could get to keep *my* spirit. Remy tossed his duffel on the floor next to me and placed his cold hands on my face.

"Hey!" I laughed, "You're an ass."

He chuckled.

"You made great time," I said.

He nodded, "Yeah…I might have been kind of pushing it too…I'm gonna get a shower, cool?"

"I thought you'd be staying with Holly," I raised an eyebrow. Remy removed his coat, hung it on the rack, and picked his bag back up.

"I'm headed over there after my shower, but we thought we might save the slumber party for another night…kids and Christmas, you know," he replied.

I nodded as he headed toward the bathroom. A few minutes later, Rhett came bounding down the stairs and into the living room. He sat next to me on the sofa, putting his arm around my shoulders. He motioned for Beegee to come from her spot where she waited for Remy. She looked from the bathroom door and back to Rhett, reluctantly obliged, hopping up next to him and he scratched her behind the ears.

"Did I hear your brother?" He asked, taking a sip from my cup.

I nodded, "Yeah, he's getting a shower and going to Holly's for a while…spend time with her and the kids."

"Good," he smiled, pulling me closer and I nuzzled in. We stared at the fireplace and watched the flames lick the grate and logs. "When's Stacia home?"

I looked at the clock, "Any time now…she said she would be home after dinner with Josh's parents."

Rhett nodded and was quiet for a moment in thought. I leaned my head on my husband's shoulder.

"What's on your mind?" I asked.

He shrugged, "Oh, I don't know…just thinking about how quiet it is around here tonight…peaceful. Hasn't been like this in a while, you know."

"True…so, is there something you want to do?" I leaned deeper into him.

"Nope. Nothing…just this," he replied. "Just this."

Epilogue

May 17

It's been six months since Mom passed away from cancer. And as we have all continued to quietly grieve her in our own way, as it does, life continues forward. In February, we were finally able to settle the rest of mom's estate, as it were. After all the life insurance policies, retirement plans with death benefits, and other financial savings, my brothers and I split a good chunk of money; three hundred and seventy-five thousand dollars, to be exact.

I put a large part of my portion back into investments and retirement for Rhett and me. With the rest, I finished paying off the loan on our home. Remy took some of his inheritance and purchased a new house for himself about three minutes away. As for Jack, well, I couldn't begin to wonder how he used his money, and I don't care. Once the final paperwork was completed, phone calls and face-to-face meetings between me and Jack were now practically nonexistent. Which is how it should be. While I loved my mother with my entire soul, I disagree with her on forcing a relationship with people just because they're blood. Blood means nothing if there isn't mutual respect and frankly, there just isn't any for Jack.

He clearly feels the same way and I'm okay with that.

As for the rest of our mother's possessions, I donated most of her clothing to homeless shelters and other charitable organizations. She would have liked that. In early March, I was finally able to comb through her jewelry, matching items to the pictures she took. What I found out in that endeavor is that my mom was a meticulous record keeper. As I opened each small box containing a piece of her treasure, I found small notes tucked inside with specifics on the piece. I knew which ones were gifts from my father, which ones were family heirlooms, and which ones she purchased herself; all of them were in her handwriting and with dates. This was something I decided to continue and have recently gone through my own collection and have done the same. I hope my kids appreciate it as much as I did. For her jewelry, I made sure to get every piece to the right person along with the signed picture to match. And yes, this was absolutely a passive-aggressive dig at my brother and no, I absolutely did not get his permission before contacting my niece, Valentine.

Fuck off, Jack.

I did, however, give my brother our grandfather's

watch. He was Granddad's namesake, after all, and damn it, my mother was right; I am the fairest. That watch was passed from my grandfather to my dad who was the oldest son of five children. I thought it only fitting for it to pass to my father's oldest son, that person being Jack. I didn't, however, want to deal with any questions regarding the rest of mom's stuff, so I made sure to deliver it and his baby book when I was positive he wasn't home. Elaine was quite shocked when she answered the door and found me standing outside.

"Oh…good morning, Jera…come in," she stepped back from the large oak door, allowing me to pass.

"Hi, Elaine," I stepped just inside the threshold and held the tattered box and the book out to her.

"Jack's not here…" she began.

I cut her short, "I know…that's why I'm here." I handed her the items.

"What's this?"

I paused and drew in a sharp breath.

"This was Granddad Jackson's watch. Dad inherited it when he died…it belongs to Jack now," I replied. Elaine smiled warmly at me. "And his baby book."

"Thank you, Jera…I know he'll appreciate this," she said.

"Well, just don't let him sell it or anything," I commented softly. She frowned at me gently and was quiet for a short moment.

"Jera, I know you and your brother haven't always seen eye to eye…"

I choked a chuckle, "That's an understatement."

"He's definitely set in his ways…but he just does what he thinks is best," she sighed. "He loves his family…including you and Jeremy."

"I think his feelings are more complicated than that," I paused. "Just, please make sure he gets them…I'd appreciate it." I turned, stepped back through the doorway, and left. I realize she's in a difficult spot, but I wasn't going to listen to her make excuses for him when he's had a lifetime to be a decent human. And I've come to terms with the end of that relationship; it didn't matter anymore.

Lastly, there was Beegee. I really hate to call Beegee a possession, but she did belong to my mother. When the time came for a decision to be made about the little Shelty, it was really a non-starter for me. Beegee had lived in my home for almost two years; this was her home too. Oddly enough, Remy didn't see it that way. In some weird twist, he really wanted her to live with him. To be honest, my initial response was to tell him hell no, Beegee would stay with me. But, while she is probably the happiest, most friendly canine to ever exist, I did recognize she and Remy had a special bond. I reluctantly agreed.

However, my brother, knowing me as well as he does, suspected I was having a difficult time letting her go and why. I mean, how could he not? She was the last living connection we had to our Mom and letting her go with him meant I was allowing that connection to be severed. So, in standard Remy fashion, he proposed a compromise: We would share Beegee in the same way an amicably divorced couple would share custody of their children. It might seem like a strange arraignment to some, but for us, it works. We split time with her every other week, and if one of us is out of town, the other gets the extra time. It's a win-win.

When April came around, I finally made the

decision to start applying for a teaching position somewhere. I'm really excited about going back to work as teaching has always been my love and passion. To date, I've had six interviews in four schools, so I think my prospects look good. Recently, I picked up a temporary, part-time job tutoring GED students which has really reignited the desire for education I thought I may have lost. Remy says he can't wait for me to go back to work so I'll stop encouraging Holly's house renovation projects.

Speaking of Remy and Holly, they've decided to get married in July. It's such an insane thought in my mind, that just a year ago, she just knew there wasn't a decent man left in this city and he was living as a hardcore nomad, convinced he'd never love again or even if he *could* be loved. Now, you can't pry them apart. Remy began running his own welding company which puts him at home and at their dinner table every night. For Ashton and Jace, this is a blessing since their father, Charlie, has only made a singular appearance in their life since Thanksgiving. Holly did a fantastic job as a single mom, but everyone needs help sometimes and Remy was more than happy to fill that role, among others. Luckily, I've always been Aunt Jera to the kids, but I'm so excited now for it to become official.

April also brought my own kids some major life-changing decisions. Harrison was finishing his second semester of college. After a lot of discussion with his dad, he decided to enlist in the Navy after graduation in a few years as he feels like it will offer him the very best career opportunities. I'm excited for him because I know he will love every minute, but as his mom, I'm nervous too; he's my baby boy, after all. Also, to our excitement, Stacia received a scholarship to play basketball with the University of Missouri, Columbia in the fall. A month before she graduated high school, we were all on hand that rainy spring day as she signed her letter of intent on the basketball court of her high school. She is on cloud nine right now and Rhett and I couldn't be more proud of her. We really are lucky parents.

Uncle Chuck and Aunt Leann are doing well, although they have been playing the part of the medical taxi service for Aunt Jean. In January, she had a small stroke that incapacitated her for several weeks. She has been pretty reluctant to leave her house much, but my uncle does a decent job of getting her out to visit doctors and family. She is still upset with me about granddad's watch, especially after I gave it to Jack as she didn't find it "appropriate".

I'm not sure how it was inappropriate either.

At any rate, Uncle Chuck seems to keep her in line most of the time when I'm around. I think he's most of all embarrassed about her behavior and I honestly feel for him. I'm sure it's not easy to be her younger brother; it certainly isn't easy being her niece.

Mom's remaining sibling, Yvonne, passed away in March. Rhett couldn't get the time off to travel, so I went to her funeral by myself. In the last year, she moved back to Kansas to be closer to her own extended family and children. I remember calling her to tell her that Mom had died. The phone was silent for a short moment when I heard her sniffle.

"Aunt Yvonne, are you alright?" I tried my hardest to keep my own tears to myself.

She sighed, "Oh, honey…I already know."

"Oh, did Jack call you?" I asked.

"No, sweetheart…I saw her last night…she told me," was her reply.

To this day, I don't understand how she knew, and I never asked her or pushed the topic again. I think I was too afraid of the answer she might give me. And I won't lie, it is a comforting thought that maybe the possibility that we are able to reach out from the beyond is there. Or maybe that's just me trying on those rose-colored glasses other people are particularly fond of; who knows?

With both of the kids officially adults and out of school, Rhett and I have decided to make the most of our summer and go on vacation together, just the two of us. We have always loved traveling but have never really gone anywhere special together in the last twenty years without the kids. A day after Remy and Holly's wedding, we are leaving on a fifteen-day road trip heading west. We plan to spend several days in San Diego and then drive up to Oceanside to visit friends we met while Rhett was stationed there. We love road trips and one of our favorite parts of living around the country was getting there; so, this is a vacation we can't wait to have and I can't wait to see the ocean again.

My mental health needs the break. It's still so hard some days to be in my house alone. I find myself making the same path through the living room, around a recliner that is no longer there. It took me all of two months to finally get to a point where I could open the door to her room without completely falling apart. Then, another month to keep her lockbox open long enough to do any kind of sorting. What I found out is that Mom kept the oddest items as keepsakes. Small things that would be trash or obscure relics to anyone else were favored mementos of happier times. She had a napkin from Jack and Kathleen's wedding. Mom always loved Kathleen. When she found out that they were divorcing, she told Jack that Kathleen would *always* be her daughter, no matter what happened between them; and she meant it.

There was the corsage from junior prom that Remy wore. It was the very first time he had ever put on a tuxedo and Mom thought he was the most handsome child she had ever laid eyes on, especially after he gave her the first dance of the evening in our small kitchen. She had snapshots of ball games, dances, and parades. Newspaper clippings of obituaries of family members and friends. But the item that made me giggle and cry simultaneously was the envelope with my name on the outside in her looping scrawl. I opened it slowly only because I was completely unsure as to what it could possibly be. What wild and weird treasure did I find inside?

An old five-dollar bill.

The memory of this envelope flooded over me like a waterfall. When I was sixteen years old, I worked as an after-school nanny for one of the doctor's Mom worked with at St. Vincent's hospital. I was paid two-hundred dollars a week to make sure his two boys, ages eight and five, did their homework, had dinner, took their bath, and were entertained until either he or his wife came home in the evening. Of that two-hundred dollars, I had to give my parents one-third of my pay to be put away for car insurance on my personal vehicle that was paid every six months. So, a little over sixty-six dollars every week went into this small, plain white envelope with my name written on it. When the time came, Mom would sit me down with the bill to show me how much of it was my responsibility. I would then take all the cash out, count out what I owed her, and pay her my portion. If there were any leftovers, they would go back into the envelope as a start for the next six-month cycle. This was a common practice in our house as Jack and Remy had their own envelopes at one time. Apparently, mine was the only one with a deposit still remaining. I put the five dollars back and tucked the envelope in the top drawer of my dresser. It will be another story I'll tell my kids someday.

Eventually, I was finally able to clean out the entire room. I gave it a fresh coat of paint, replaced her decor, and purchased new bedding for the queen-sized bed. That room will always remind me of my Mom; nothing will change that, and I don't want it to. What I needed was for it to provide different memories so I could move forward. Remy moved into the space for a while before he and Holly sold her house and purchased the new one. New memories were made. Harrison has decided he would like the space now as it has a private outside entrance and a lot more room than his current bedroom. Rhett and I both agreed it would offer him more privacy, which is something a young man needs. I wish my Mom could be here to see all the changes that have taken place. I know she would be so proud of how everyone is doing.

I know there will always be an empty place in my heart for her. The pain of losing someone, especially one that you are so close to, is at times indescribable and debilitating. You lose your breath, you cry, and you get angry at their absence. I do believe, however, that our souls never cease to exist, even on this plane. I somehow know she is still with me, even today.

Whether it's in someone else's laugh, a familiarity in the way another person walks, or even catching a whiff of the perfume she wore on occasion, I know she is there.

She was the greatest, most devoted, most caring, badass woman to ever exist. She was as beautiful and loving as she was strong. She moved through life with the grace of an angel. Not the ethereal kind from imagination, but a real, honest, warrior of old whose armor was splattered in mud and blood from a long battle that was fought and won. She was uncommonly good and true. Her laughter rang from the mountains bringing joy to all that heard it. Her personality was fiery. Her love for everyone she met was deep and never-ending.

And I got to call her Mom.

About the Author

January Kelly is a longtime writer and holds a BS in Sociology with an interest in Religious Studies. She is an avid reader of fantasy and science fiction and a lover of all genres of music. January is based in the wilds of the Missouri Midwest where she loves to embroider bad words on bookmarks, have cocktails and queso with her friends, and go on long walks with her husband, Jarritt.

Social media links

https://www.januarykelly.com

https://www.facebook.com/profile.php?id=100067850730415

Don't miss these exciting works by January
Kelly...

Hidden Intent
The Hidden, Book 1

**They want Derek for who he is; Derek wants her
for what she is.**

When Derek Argent falls victim to an obsessive
Succubus, he and his closest friend, Siobhan, struggle
to figure out why.

Survival is the game and secrets are the price of
admission. Can uncovering his past help Derek save
the woman he loves?

Smoke and Shadow
The Hidden, Book 2

**Derek and Siobhan have waited months to be
together, but someone has other plans.**

When Arvendon is attacked by an unknown assailant
that allows a former vampire queen to go free, The
Hidden is left to pick up the pieces…and their dead.

A rising Changeling army. A former vampire queen
on the run. Is it possible for the Hidden to survive?
Or will it crumble into civil war?

The Last Lament of the Late Shawn Reilly

Shawn went through hell for her happily ever after. Why is it falling apart now?

Shawn Reilly has lived a delicate life of devastating loss and profound happiness. An award-winning actress, she's become a master of putting on an act to cover the hidden pain.

With her reality crumbling around her, she faces her darkest moments.

Can she accept what fate is leading her to and finally get back what she lost long ago? Or will she slip into darkness?

www.ingramcontent.com/pod-product-compliance
Lightning Source LLC
Chambersburg PA
CBHW020154310726
48970CB00006B/2141